About the author

A.D. Burlace is a twenty-five year old, originally from south London. This is his first book, which he has been writing since he was thirteen years old. He loves writing books, screenplays and films. His interests are history, rescuing animals (of which he has many), and spending time with his close family.

SEA OF DECEPTION

A.D. Burlace

SEA OF DECEPTION

Vanguard Press

VANGUARD PAPERBACK

© Copyright 2018
A.D. Burlace

The right of A.D. Burlace to be identified as author of
this work has been asserted by him in accordance with the
Copyright, Designs and Patents Act 1988.

All Rights Reserved

No reproduction, copy or transmission of this publication
may be made without written permission.
No paragraph of this publication may be reproduced,
copied or transmitted save with the written permission of the
publisher, or in accordance with the provisions
of the Copyright Act 1956 (as amended).

Any person who commits any unauthorised act in relation to
this publication may be liable to criminal
prosecution and civil claims for damages.

A CIP catalogue record for this title is
available from the British Library.

ISBN 978 1 784653 29 3

*Vanguard Press is an imprint of
Pegasus Elliot MacKenzie Publishers Ltd.*
www.pegasuspublishers.com

First Published in 2018

**Vanguard Press
Sheraton House Castle Park
Cambridge England**

Printed & Bound in Great Britain

Acknowledgements

I would like to acknowledge my mum, without whom this book would never have been finished.

Dedicated to Auntie Lee. You will always be missed.

Prologue

The early 18th century was a time of extreme violence. War ravaged the lands, and pirates made the seas a treacherous place to navigate whilst the coasts of England seemed a safe place, far from the conflict and unrest that was engulfing the globe, in the quiet of a small village in southern England, I would hear a story of a young boy who would grow into a hero. As navies fought and armies fell, he would never stop in his quest. A quest that would take him to the most hostile places, introduce him to the most dangerous people and learn that swords and pistols were not the most dangerous weapons.

Chapter 1

Our story starts in England in the year 1703, in a small village just outside the town of Southampton a small boy, whose name was Jack Leighton, was out playing in the woods, just outside of the village with his best friend Edward Rosley. They were playing hide and seek when a flash of lightning streaked across the sky moments later came a mighty crash of thunder. From the direction of the village came running a young girl; it was Jack's twelve-year-old sister Elizabeth.

"Jack," she called, "Mother wants you to come home!"

Jack replied, "All right, Elizabeth, coming!"

The boys then turned and started towards home, with Elizabeth skipping ahead.

On the way home it started to rain; at first it was a light shower but as they got closer to the village it started to pour. The boys started to run, with lightning flashing through the sky around them and the sound of thunder echoing all around.

As they got closer to their homes they shouted to each other, "see you tomorrow," and with that they went to their houses. When Jack came through the door of his house, there standing in the small passageway stood his mother, Catherine; an elegant woman with long flowing brown hair.

"Where have you been? You're soaking wet and freezing cold." She said, grabbing a blanket from in front of the fire and wrapping it around Jack and cuddling him to warm him up.

"I've been out playing with Edward in the woods," Jack replied, smiling.

"All right then," Catherine replied as she started to dry his long brown hair, "There that's better," she said putting the dripping wet blanket back by the fire to dry.

***

Two hours later, just as the sun was starting to set, the door opened and in came Jack's father, Henry. A tall muscular man with dark hair and a beard, soaking wet and covered in a fine dusting of sawdust.

"Good evening, my darling," he said, removing his soaked woolen jumper and placing it to dry by the open fire. He turned around to greet his wife with a passionate kiss, then turned to greet his son with a ruffling of his hair and a pat on the shoulder. "So what have you been up to today my son?"

"Just been out playing with Edward in the woods father" he said with a twinkle in his eye.

"I hope you have been keeping out of trouble," his father replied with a cheeky smile.

"Yes, Father I have," Jack replied smiling back. Henry then turned and hugged Elizabeth. "And what have you been getting up to, my beautiful daughter?"

"I have been helping Mother," she replied with a cheeky smile.

As they sat at the table in front of the fire, Catherine walked in carrying a large pot; she placed it on the table and a wonderful aroma arose from it.

She dished up four bowls. "Come on now, eat up."

***

After supper, Catherine took the bowls and the pot out into the kitchen. Whilst she was gone Henry leaned in close to Jack and said, "You know your birthday is in a few days so, I am going to take you out and teach you how to fight with sword and pistol."

"Thank you, Father" Jack replied.

"Can I come?" piped up Elizabeth.

"Not until you are older, my beautiful girl."

"Oh..." Elizabeth pouted, then walked away.

Catherine then came back into the room. "All right you two. Time for bed."

"OK, Mother," Jack and Elizabeth said, standing up and hugging their father good night.

As Catherine covered Jack over she kissed him on the forehead and said "Good night," then she turned and walked into Elizabeth's room, tucked her in and kissed her goodnight. As she left she blew out the candle. Catherine walked down the stairs and into the room where Henry was sitting by the fire.

She sat down next to him and looking into his eyes asked him, "How was your day?"

"Good," "he replied, "except..."

"Except what?" she asked, concerned.

"Well, when I was in the woods attempting to fell a huge oak tree, I heard this sound like a ship's cannon, but I could not see any flashes."

"Maybe it was just branches falling." Catherine said quietly.

"Maybe," Henry replied. But as he said it a flash of doubt entered his mind.

"What else could it be?" Catherine said, as she saw the concern on his face.

Henry looked away, and then back towards her, his face solemn as the words left his mouth. "I do not know, my love."

Catherine looked at him and said, "I would not worry, it is probably nothing."

"You are probably right," Henry replied, smiling gently at her.

Catherine smiled back and said, "It's over now, so I wouldn't worry yourself."

Then without uttering any more words he lay down by the fire, placing his head softly on the floor. Catherine followed, placing her head gently on his chest. They both drifted off into a deep sleep.

***

The next day Henry was out in the forest chopping down a huge oak tree, but the thought of what he had heard the night before played on his mind. That evening Henry came in late. Catherine, Elizabeth and Jack were already asleep so Henry quietly went upstairs and got into bed next to Catherine and fell into a deep sleep still thinking of what he had heard the day before.

CHAPTER 2

The following morning as the sun rose gently in the sky, Henry and Catherine awoke. As they slowly rose to their feet, they noticed it was deathly quiet. No birds, no wind, no sounds. They thought that it was just early, and that there would be no one up at this time.

Catherine went to make breakfast, which was a bowl of hot oats. While she was cooking, Henry went to wake Jack and Elizabeth.

"Good morning, my children," he called out in the hallway.

"Good morning, Father," they replied. Jack sat up whilst yawning and rubbing his eyes; Elizabeth jumped out of her bed and gave her father a hug. Henry then went into Jack's room.

"Time for breakfast, we have a big day ahead," Henry said, with a twinkle in his eye.

"Yes, Father," Jack replied, as his father was leaving the room. Jack got out of his bed and got dressed. They then went downstairs where their mother gave them a bowl of hot oats each. After eating breakfast, Jack and his father put on their boots and walked outside.

"Bye, Mother, bye Elizabeth see you later!"

"See you soon, my love," Henry said to his wife as he was walking away.

"Goodbye, my loves, be safe," called Catherine.

***

"Where are we going?" said Jack to his father.

"You'll see soon, my boy," said Henry walking with him to the blacksmiths. On the way they ran into Edward and his father, Joseph.

"Hello, Jack," said Edward.

"Hello, Edward".

"What are you two doing out here today?" William asked.

"Just going to the village to get my boy a present." Henry replied.

"What's the occasion?" said William.

"It's my son's birthday tomorrow and he's fifteen, so I wanted to start his training," Henry replied, beaming.

"We'll walk together," said Jack and they all started to walk towards the blacksmith's.

***

"Morning, James, do you have a sword for my son?" said Henry.

"Let's see," said James reaching for a rapier with beautiful gilding at the top and around the hilt.

"Try this," said James, handing the sword to Henry. Henry gave the sword to Jack

"How does it feel?" asked Henry.

"Wonderful, it is really light and balanced, I love it," said Jack, a smile beaming across his face, he handed the sword back to his father.

"How much is it?" asked Henry holding the sword.

"One guinea," replied James.

"How about eighteen shillings?"

James smiled and said, "You drive a hard bargain, sir," he paused.

"You have a deal," he said, shaking Henry's hand. Henry counted out eight shillings and handed James the money, then he turned and presented Jack with the sword.

"Thank you," said Jack, attaching the sword to his belt.

"I know your birthday is not until tomorrow, but you deserve it, now come on Son, we have things to do". Jack turned to his friend. "Goodbye" he said.

"Goodbye," replied Edward.

Henry put his hand out and shook his friend Joseph's hand, and said, "Goodbye."

As Henry and Jack were walking, Jack turned to his father "Where are we going now Father?"

"You will see soon, my son," Henry replied.

***

They seemed to have walked for ages when they came to the gunsmith.

"Good morning, do you have a long pistol for my son?" Henry asked politely.

"Yes, try this one," the gunsmith passed the pistol to Henry, who then passed Jack the pistol.

"How does that feel, my boy?" asked Henry.

Jack held his arm out in front and closed one eye. "It is excellent, Father," Jack replied, looking at the pistol with a grin from ear to ear, then he handed it back to his father.

"How much, sir?" Henry asked.

"One pound sterling," the gunsmith replied.

"That seems quite fair," replied Henry and paid the gunsmith.

"Thank you, sir" and they said goodbye.

***

Henry and Jack turned for home, Jack now looking more like a soldier than a young man. When they arrived at the house,

Jack opened the door and called to his mother. "We're home!"

Catherine turned around and said, "How did it go?"

"Excellent! Look what Father has got me," Jack said, showing off his sword and his pistol.

"Oh, my goodness!" Catherine replied.

"It's OK, Mother, it's not loaded," Jack said.

"Oh, thank goodness," she replied, sounding relieved.

"Tomorrow I'll teach you how to use them safely," said Henry with a warm smile.

***

That night after dinner Jack was lying in bed. His father began telling him about his first lesson with a sword.

"I remember it like it was yesterday," he began, "my father told me, if you get stabbed or sliced you are doing it wrong. Those words have stuck with me and now I have passed them on to you."

"So what happened the first time you and your father practiced?"

Henry chuckled. "He knocked me on my backside, pointed his sword at me and said you're not much good down there so I got up and this time when I made a mistake he sliced my trousers so they fell down! He was laughing up until Mother saw but do not worry I will not do that to you. Now go to sleep; we have a big day tomorrow."

Henry said, "Goodnight," and blew out the lamp. Then he turned and went in to Elizabeth's room, but she was already asleep, so he covered her over and walked out of her room, blowing out the candle in the lamp as he left. Then he went into the other bedroom where Catherine was already asleep, he got into bed beside her and said gently "Goodnight, my love."

He kissed her softly on the cheek. She stirred slightly but didn't wake.

***

The next morning was the 22nd of May. Jack awoke to see his sister standing by the bed with a look of concern on her face.
"What's wrong, Jack? Are you all right?" Elizabeth asked.
"Yes why?" he replied.
"You were tossing and turning in your sleep," she said.
"I was having a bad dream," said Jack, sitting up smiling, "Let's go and have some breakfast."
They went downstairs. Henry was already sitting at the table. He beckoned them over.
Standing up, he kissed Elizabeth on the forehead and squeezed Jack on his shoulder and said, "After breakfast, we shall begin our training."
"Morning, dears," said Catherine, coming in from the kitchen, kissing Henry on the lips and then Jack and Elizabeth on their heads.
"Morning, Mother," they both replied.
After breakfast Henry turned to Jack and said "Come on Son, time to go."
They both got up and as they reached the door they both said goodbye to Catherine and Elizabeth, who both turned, smiled and replied, "Goodbye, you two, be careful."

***

Outside, Henry showed Jack how to hold a sword and how to fight without getting hurt.
"All right, let's start with the position of your feet," said Henry, putting his right foot forward and drawing his sword, "Now, you try."

Jack, standing next to his father, put his right foot forward and drew his brand new sword and raised it to about waist height.

"Like this?" Jack asked.

"Raise your sword a little higher, just above your waist," Henry said, walking over and adjusting Jack's arm, "Like that, now follow my lead."

Henry then showed Jack a series of moves, starting with a slice and finishing with a thrust. "Now, take it slowly, one motion at a time."

Jack then copied each move, although, half the speed of his father.

"That's great, Son. The speed will come the more you practice."

As the sun was setting, Jack and Henry started home. By the time they arrived home the sun had set and night was upon them. They went inside and were greeted by Catherine.

"Evening, dears," she said, kissing Jack on the cheek and Henry on the lips.

Jack yawned. "Good night, Father," he said and went upstairs to his room.

"Good night, Son," Henry replied. He went upstairs and entered his and Catherine's room where she was awake waiting for him. As he got undressed and got into bed he gazed into her beautiful blue eyes, then passionately kissed her. They embraced and made love in front of the dim crackling fire.

Chapter 3

Over the coming weeks Jack's skills with a blade vastly improved. On the last day of the first week in June, Jack and Henry were practicing out near the woods that they were so fond of.

After they had finished Henry said, "Well done, my boy, you're in fine form. Over the next few months I'll teach you how to use that pistol properly, safely and quickly. Remember: a fast reload can mean the difference between life and death."

Later on, after dinner, Jack was lying in bed when he heard his parents talking, though too quietly for him to make out what they were saying. After the voices had died down, Catherine came into Elizabeth's room to check on her. Elizabeth was already fast asleep. She then went into Jack's room; Jack was just dozing.

"Don't forget about your sister's birthday tomorrow. She will be thirteen – I hope you will get her a nice gift."

"Yes, I will, Mother," he answered as he drifted off into a deep sleep.

***

The next day was the 8th June; Jack was awoken by an excitable Elizabeth.

"Wake up, wake up Jack!" she exclaimed.

"All right, Elizabeth," Jack replied, still half asleep.

After breakfast, Jack took Elizabeth to the clearing where he had been the day before with his father.

"What are we doing here?" Elizabeth asked.

"I'm getting your gift," Jack said as he walked over to a large oak tree. Jack bent over and picked up part of a branch.

"It doesn't look like much," said Elizabeth.

"It will do, just give me time," replied Jack, smiling.

"All right," she said, and the two of them started off home. When they arrived home Elizabeth went inside the house while Jack sat outside, found a sharp knife and began whittling away at the branch until it resembled a small shield with a horse carving on the front. Once he had finished, he went inside and presented the little shield to Elizabeth saying, "This will keep you safe; you must always keep it with you."

"Thank you," said Elizabeth, giving Jack a kiss on the cheek.

The family all said "happy birthday" in unison to Elizabeth.

CHAPTER 4

As the days and months rolled by the weather got colder and colder and the leaves turned from green to a beautiful golden colour. As the days got longer so too did Jack's practice sessions. One chilly September morning, Jack and Henry were out practicing in their favourite spot.

"Keep your guard up, my boy. Remember parry then follow up with an attack," said Henry, demonstrating on the make shift dummy he had made out of an old scarecrow. "Now you, just like that."

"OK, Father," Jack replied, replicating the moves his father had just showed him.

"Now, let's try that with a target that fights back," Henry said, readying his sword,

"On guard!" exclaimed Jack, lunging forward, his sword shining in the slowly-setting sun the sound of the swords clashing echoed through the nearby woods as Jack and Henry's practice battle commenced. Jack's guard fell slightly and Henry moved to knock the sword from his hand, seeing the advantage. As he swung he caught Jack's hand causing a deep wound on the side of it. Jack with the pain of the wound written across his face, switched the sword into his other hand.

"I can still fight," he said, his lip trembling and tears filling his eyes.

"No, we need to see to that wound," Henry said with a look of concern, coming towards Jack.

"No, I can fight," Jack said raising his sword, now in his left hand and changing his stance.

"OK, Son, but afterwards we are going to get that hand looked at," Henry said with a slight smile on his face, partly out of pride, partly thinking this was going to be easy, not knowing that Jack had been practicing on his left with Edward for fun. Jack made the first move, this time remaining completely silent. The blood dripped from his right hand Henry parried but Jack quickly followed up with three carefully timed moves that not only disarmed Henry but put him on the ground looking at the tip of Jack's sword.

"Well done, my boy, you've won! Now let's go and get that hand sorted," Henry said, getting to his feet and taking Jack's hand. He tore a piece of cloth from his jacket and wrapped the wound tightly. "Come on!"

Henry took hold of Jacks left wrist and led Jack to the blacksmith.

As they approached Henry called out, "James!"

"Yes?" came the reply.

"We need your help."

"What with?"

"We need your poker and your furnace – we have a wound here."

"All right, come and sit here, son," James said pointing at a tree stump. Henry led Jack to the stump as Jack was quite weary by now. Jack took a seat.

"Now this might sting a little," James said, unwrapping Jack's hand.

Henry took off his belt and gave it to Jack and said, "Bite down on this."

Henry noticed James give him the nod, at which point he grabbed Jack's shoulders and pinned him down to the stump. While James grabbed the poker from the furnace, he grabbed Jack's hand and applied the white hot tip to the wound instantly cauterizing it, Jack let out a muffled scream then passed out. When he came to he was laying on the floor. Henry and James looked down at him.

"Are you all right my boy?" Henry said, reaching out his hand.

Jack took his hand and Henry helped him to his feet.

"Ah, what happened?" Jack asked, his voice rough.

"It's all right, Son, we cauterized the wound and stopped the bleeding – you'll be fine as long as you don't contract an infection, so we bandaged your hand as well with fresh linens."

"Now, you take it easy," James said, waving as Jack and Henry walked away.

"Thank you," called Jack.

As they approached home Jack collapsed.

"Are you all right, my boy?" Henry exclaimed rushing over to him.

"Yes I'm fine, just feeling a bit unwell."

Henry helped Jack to his feet and then put Jack's arm round his shoulder. Jack then put his arm round Henry.

"Come on, Son, nearly home."

As they entered the home, Catherine greeted them.

"Hello, my darlings, how was practice... Oh my goodness! What happened to your hand?" she gasped, running over to Jack. "Oh! My poor boy." She turned and glared at Henry, "WHAT HAPPENED?" Anger laced her voice.

"We were practicing fighting and I caught Jack's hand, accidentally."

Catherine grabbed Jack, hugging him tightly, a tear in her eye. "Come sit down." She led him over to the fire. "Now, you just sit there and warm up while I finish dinner."

"Thank you, Mother," Jack replied.

Catherine smiled, then turned and left the room. As she left, Elizabeth came skipping into the room.

"Hi, Jack," she said smiling, then skipped back out of the room after her mother.

"You did well today, Son and when your hand is better I will teach you more about using that pistol. We haven't practiced enough with it yet, but for now you must rest," Henry said, ruffling Jacks hair. Jack then went upstairs, laid down and fell asleep.

***

A few weeks passed, and now it was October. Jack's hand had healed and he had begun his lessons again. One morning, Jack awoke and went downstairs to find his father so they could begin training. Elizabeth was already there eating her breakfast.

"Where's Father?" Jack asked his mother.

Catherine turned. "He's gone to work; the navy is building a new ship and your father is the best lumberjack in the south so he's been employed to cut down oak trees for timber."

"Wow! A new ship… I wonder what it will be called."

"Well, your father is taking you to see the ships launch, while your sister and I run some errands."

"Thank you, that will be wonderful."

Jack finished his breakfast then got dressed and headed for the door. "Bye Mother, I'm going to go see Edward."

"Be good and be safe," she replied.

"Bye, Elizabeth."

***

Jack left and walked to Edward's home. He knocked on the door, Edward answered.

"Hello Jack, how are you?"

"Not bad. My hand still hurts a bit."

"Is that the excuse you're going to use when I beat you then?" laughed Edward.

Jack smirked and said, "I might have to."

Edward said goodbye to his mother then closed the door. The two boys started walking.

"So you up for a game of lefty?" said Jack.

"Aah so that's your plan," grinned Edward. They stopped at their favourite clearing just outside the forest; the sounds of axes hitting trees echoed around them with giant thuds. The boys drew their swords and put them in their left hands.

"Ready," said Jack.

"Ready," replied Edward.

"On guard!" yelled Jack.

Edward made the first move; thrusting, which was quickly deflected by Jack who had a big grin on his face. Jack replied with a combination of moves at the now laughing Edward. The two of them exchanged blows for an hour, laughing the whole time. The two friends had never been happier.

After they had finished, they walked to Edward's home. As Edward went into his home, Jack waved and turned towards his home. As he arrived at the door he turned and saw the orange sky and the sun setting behind the trees. 'What a beautiful view' he thought. He opened the door and went inside.

***

The weeks went by and as the weather got colder the leaves had all but gone; only a few brown ones remained. Henry had been paid handsomely for all the timber he had supplied to the navy for the new ship HMS Revenge; a seventy gun, third-rate ship of the line.

On the final delivery Jack went with him and saw the launch at Portsmouth. He stared in awe at the giant wooden hull of the ship.

"She's beautiful," gasped Jack,

"Yes, she is and I'm proud that a little bit of me is in her," replied Henry.

Then as everyone cheered, the mighty hull slid down the slipway and in to the sea.

"Come on, Son, it's a long way home."

Jack and Henry started the long trip home.

***

A day later they arrived back home, tired. They went in, had dinner, then went straight to bed. The next day Henry took Jack out to the shooting range he had made.

"All right son, load your pistol as quick as you can because it could save your life!"

Jack drew his pistol, took a cartridge, and tore off the top, holding the ball in his hand. He poured a tiny bit of powder in the pan then closed the frizzen. Then he poured the rest of the powder down the barrel followed quickly by the ball which was placed in a small piece of cloth. He then pulled the ram rod out and rammed the ball down the barrel, replaced the ram rod, pulled the flintlock back, aimed and fired! The sound echoed around the forest. They then looked at the target and to Henry's surprise Jack had not only hit the target, he had hit close to the bulls eye.

"Well done, Son, that was quick and accurate I don't think there's anything more I can teach you!"

"Thank you, Father."

"It's getting dark! Time for us to go home."

CHAPTER 5

The months had rolled by and it was now May 22nd 1704. It was Jack's sixteenth birthday. He was awakened in the early hours of the morning by his little sister Elizabeth, bouncing around shouting, "Happy birthday, happy birthday!"

Jack rubbed the sleep from his eyes and looked out of the window. He noticed that the sun was just coming over the horizon. He immediately looked back at Elizabeth and smiled, then laid back down to try and go back to sleep, but as his eyes began to close, he felt his sisters tiny hands on his shoulders.

She started to shake him. "How can you sleep, it's your birthday!" and with that she pulled off his blanket.

"All right," sighed Jack and slowly rose to his feet. He dressed and they both went downstairs for breakfast.

After breakfast, Catherine gave Jack a small amulet with the words **Sercurus sol mea**.

"Thank you," Jack gasped, looking closely at the word engraved in the circle of gold.

Catherine smiled. "My Father gave it to me and his Father gave it to him. The words mean stay safe, my son."

Jack slipped the gold chain over his head with a smile.

"I never had any brothers, so my Father said it was to be given to my son on his sixteenth birthday." With that, Catherine gave Jack a massive hug.

"Where's Father?" asked Jack, looking around.

Catherine's face changed. "He's gone to Portsmouth, he'll be back later."

"All right, Mother." Jack then turned and was about to leave when Elizabeth came running up.

"Here you are," as she placed a stone in the shape of a ship's hull into his hand.

"Thank you Elizabeth, it looks like the one that Father supplied the wood for."

"You're welcome!" she smiled, and with that Elizabeth turned and ran off.

***

Jack left the house, and went and found Edward.

"Happy birthday my friend," he said cheerfully.

"Thank you," replied Jack and the two of them went off to their favourite practice spot. They practiced throughout the day, and as the sun started to set, the two friends said their goodbyes and went to their respective homes.

Jack came through the door to find his mother crying and holding Henry tightly.

"What is the matter?" asked Jack.

"I have been called up to serve in the army," Henry replied solemnly.

"Where are you going?" asked Elizabeth.

"I am going from here to Portsmouth to join the Duke of Marlborough's forces in Germany."

"Will you be gone long Father?" asked Jack.

"I don't know, but it is my honour to serve my country like my father before me," Henry replied. "But that's enough doom and gloom; it's Jack's birthday!"

And with that, they all sat down and had dinner, talking and laughing.

After dinner Catherine tucked Elizabeth in, then Jack.

"Happy birthday," she said with a smile, and kissed him on the forehead.

Catherine then went into her bedroom where Henry was already waiting. She sat on the bed and with tears in her eyes said, "Do you really have to go?"

"Yes, my love, I do."

"But do you want to go?"

"You know that I don't." Henrys face changed as he said the words, to a softer gentler look. He then walked over to her, sat next to her, then they embraced.

Catherine looked into his eyes and said gently, "We had better make the most of tonight then."

She stood up and got undressed. Henry stood up to face her, looked into her eyes. Then, cupping her face in his hands gently kissed her passionately on the lips. The two of them made passionate love until the early hours of the morning, then fell asleep in each other's arms.

***

As the sun rose, and the fire had died down, Catherine awoke. She sat up, looked round and on the pillow next to her was a note. It read:

My darling love, I did not want to wake you as you looked so peaceful and saying goodbye would have been too painful. You will be in my heart and the thought of you will keep me going. All my love, Henry

CHAPTER 6

Three months had passed since Henry had left. Letters had arrived every two weeks until the second week in August. Catherine was waiting for the usual letter, when a man dressed in uniform approached on horseback.

He reached in to his bag then gave a letter to Catherine. "My condolences, Madam."

He then turned mounted his horse and rode away. Catherine opened the letter, her hands shaking. As she began to read, tears started streaming down her face.

"What's wrong, Mother?" asked Jack.

Catherine turned, her face pale. "I'm afraid that your father has been killed in action."

Jack took the letter and began reading, hoping in his mind that his mother was wrong. The letter read:

Dear Madam, I regret to inform you that your husband has been killed in battle. His death was not in vain as it helped to ensure our victory. Yours, the Duke of Marlborough.

Jack folded up the letter and gave his mother a hug, with tears beginning to form in his eyes.

"How will we tell Elizabeth?" he asked.

"I don't know," Catherine replied, still weeping.

"It will be all right," he said as Catherine squeezed him tightly.

"Thank you," she said softly.

***

That evening dinner was unusually quiet.

"What's wrong?" Elizabeth asked, looking firstly at Jack who looked at her then at his mother. Catherine smiled, then burst into tears.

"Elizabeth," Jack said, taking his sisters hand. "Father is having to stay in the army."

"But why?" she asked.

"Because he is really important," Jack replied, the lie staining his brain and leaving a bitter taste in his mouth, as he remembered his Father's words from when he was a child: "Always be honest and chivalrous and you will be successful and loved!"

The words echoed around his head, but deep down he knew it was the right thing to do.

***

As Jack and Elizabeth got ready for bed, Catherine entered the room and first tucked in Elizabeth, "Goodnight" she said kissing her on the forehead.

"Goodnight, Mother," Elizabeth replied, then she drifted off to sleep.

Catherine then turned to Jack and as she tucked him in she said, "Thank you."

"But I lied."

"No, you protected your sister. Your Father would be proud."

Jack just smiled and then drifted off to sleep.

A couple of hours later, Jack was awoken by the sound of weeping. He got up and went into his mother's room. There on the bed was Catherine with her head in her hands crying.

Catherine looked up. "What are you doing up?"

"I heard crying, so I came to see if you were all right."

"You're a good boy, thank you. I will be all right."

Jack walked over and hugged his mother. "It will be all right."

"I know, now go back to bed or you will be tired in the morning."

"All right, Mother." And with that. Jack went back to bed and drifted off to sleep.

Chapter 7

Two days later Jack was awoken by his mother and told to put on his nicest clothes. Jack didn't question why as in his mind he already knew. They set off into the village.
"Where are we going?" asked Elizabeth.

"We are going to church," replied Jack.

"Why?"

"Because they are going to hold a special service to show their respects for what Father and all the other men who were in the war did."

They entered the church and took their seats. The service was short but meaningful and after about an hour it was over. As they left, Catherine had tears in her eyes and asked Jack to take Elizabeth home.

"Why? Where are you going, Mother?"

"I'll be along shortly," replied Catherine as she turned and walked away towards the graveyard.

Jack took Elizabeth by the hand and the two set off for home. Catherine entered the graveyard and walked near a headstone towards the middle. She stopped and knelt down crying. On the headstone it read: Here lies Henry who fell in battle 13th August 1704. Loving husband to Catherine and devoted father to Jack and Elizabeth.

Later, after supper, as the sun began to set, Jack and Elizabeth were playing peacefully as their mother returned and said it was time for bed.

As the light disappeared completely from the room, Jack lay awake thinking of his father when a strange glow came from the woods. Jack thought it was just one of the locals coming home late until he heard the sound of muffled singing. He got up and looked out of the window where to his horror he saw a group of dark shadows approaching his village! As they drew closer he could see the glint of swords illuminated by the full moon.

Quick as a flash, Jack turned and ran into his mother's room and shook her, calling, "Mother! Mother!" a tone of alarm in his voice.

"What is it Jack?"

Jack, shaking with fright said, stuttering, "Men. With swords outside my window."

Catherine jumped out of her bed and raced into Jack's room and up to his window, where she saw a tall figure standing, his face covered by the shadow of his hat. As she looked, the figure slowly raised his head until just an evil smile could be seen. Catherine jumped back from the window as the figure outside said in a loud booming voice, "Have fun boys!"

Catherine turned and told Jack to wake Elizabeth, as she grabbed her late husband's sword which she kept under her bed. Jack came in with Elizabeth who was rubbing her eyes and still half asleep.

"What's happening, Mother?" Elizabeth said, yawning.

"It's going to be all right. You just stay with your brother," replied Catherine quickly. From outside, a loud cheer arose.

Catherine rushed the children downstairs towards the front door as screams and the sounds of battle reverberated from around the village. As they were half way down. Jack stopped; remembering he had forgotten something, he turned around and ran back upstairs into his room. Reaching under his bed, he grabbed the sword and pistol that his father had given him. Racing down the stairs he clambered to get his belt on and clip his sword and pistol to it. As he arrived back with his mother and sister, there came a crash of glass and a loud pounding on the back door.

Catherine opened the front door then turned to Jack. "Take your sister and keep her safe."

"Mother, you're coming too."

Catherine just smiled at him.

"Mother," replied Jack, a tear in his eye.

"Promise me you'll take care of your sister."

"I promise, Mother," Jack replied, trying not to cry.

"I'm proud of you both and I love you," Catherine said, pushing them out the door, just as the back door gave with a mighty crash and two men came charging through.

"'Allo, sweetie," one of them said.

"Go!" shouted Catherine, turning to face the men and slamming the door behind her.

"Mother!" cried Jack, unsheathing his sword and pounding on the door with all his might. He heard the sound of swords clashing; he backed away from the door looking for another way in, but the way round the house was blocked by fire. He heard the blood curdling scream of his mother followed by a thud and then silence.

The same voice muffled through the door saying, "You idiot, we wanted a fun one not a fighter."

Jack slumped against the door and put his head in his hands. He felt an anger come over him he lifted his head and then felt a hand.

"Jack, I'm scared," said Elizabeth.

"It will be all right," replied Jack, standing up. He heard a cry as one of the men from the house charged him. Jack startled, managed to block the attack and then got his footing. Remembering what his father had taught him, he dispatched the man in no time.

"That was for my mother," said Jack. He turned around to check on Elizabeth but she was nowhere to be seen. Jack started frantically looking around for her and that's when he saw all the bodies littered around him, most of the village was on fire; the sound of swords clashing and guns going off could be heard all around him. Jack headed towards the village centre when he saw Edward coming backwards out of his house locked in a duel with another man. His house on fire, his father's body in the front garden. Jack was about to go and help when he heard an "arrrrrrr!"

He spun around to see a large man charging him; a large two-handed sword above his head. Jack took a deep breath:

"I don't have time for this," he said to himself. Then the man was upon him. Jack dodged the blow, slashing as he dodged. The large man looked down at the blood, now coming from a wound across his abdomen – he snarled at Jack who thrust his sword through the man's side. The man fell forward, dead. That's when Jack noticed the tattoo on the man's back; it was a skull and cross bones.

Pirates, he thought. Jack then turned and saw Edward had killed his attacker. Jack ran up to him. "Edward, are you all right?"

"Yes, my friend, apart from my family being murdered. What about you?"

"Mother's dead and I have lost Elizabeth."

"I am sorry. I will help you find Elizabeth."

"Thank you."

Edward headed for the blacksmith while Jack went towards the woods knowing his sister had seen him playing there. As he made his way towards the woods he found the shield he had given her on the floor. He picked it up then called out, "Elizabeth!"

He saw a large figure running deep into the woods carrying a young girl. Jack charged after him. As he got closer he saw it was Elizabeth on the pirate's shoulder. Jack closed in on the pirate. When he was almost there another figure stepped out from behind a tree. Jack stopped. The figure put up his hand and the large man stopped.

"Give.Me.Back.My. Sister!" Jack snarled at the figure.

"You want her? Come and get her," said the figure. Jack started towards him, his sword still dripping with blood. Jack was now close enough to see details. The pirate leader had a light blue coat and a black hat.

"I'll kill you for what you have done to my family and my village." Jack's voice laced with pure hatred.

The pirate leader laughed as he drew his sword. The two began circling each other when Jack saw the large man begin to move.

"No!" said the pirate leader. "This one's mine." With that they charged at each other, their swords meeting with an almighty clang! It was so loud that Edward heard it and started making his way towards the forest.

Jack stared into the pirate's dark-green eyes as the swords were locked together.

"Interesting. You're not afraid," the pirate leader said in a low voice.

"I will never fear you," replied jack. With that he backed off then swung at the leaders head. The pirate leader ducked and kicked Jack's leg out from under him. Jack hit the floor with a thud. Winded, he tried to get to his feet but before he could the pirate leader had stepped on his wrist; Jack reached across trying to free it but the pirate kicked his hand away then bent down and picked up Jack's sword. Jack, thinking quickly, reached down and grabbed his pistol. Cocking it, and he fired. The pirate leader let out a roar, clutching his ear and reeling backwards. Jack scrambled to his feet, clutching his sword, staring at the pirate leader as blood ran down his face. He hit him with the hilt of his sword, Jack stumbled then the pirate leader punched him, knocking him to the floor. Jack tried to sit up but the pirate leader put his boot on Jack's chest pinning him to the ground.

"You don't give up, do you?" the pirate leader said, chuckling.

"And since you left me with a memory of you, I'll leave you with one of me." And with that, the pirate leader took his sword and began carving an upside-down triangle into Jack's right cheek. Jack let out a scream then passed out.

"We will meet again," said the pirate leader as he turned and walked away with the large pirate following him carrying Elizabeth.

Chapter 8

"Jack, Jack wake up, please."

Jack slowly opened his eyes and saw Edward kneeling beside him.

"Elizabeth!" Jack cried, trying to sit up.

Edward put his hand on his chest, stopping him. "Wait a minute, I haven't finishing bandaging your face."

"Thank you, my friend."

After Edward had finished, he helped Jack to his feet; Jack looked around and found his sword. He picked it up and sheathed it. "We have to find and alert the guards."

"But the nearest post is in Portsmouth; that's a six hour trip by horse."

"Then we had better get going."

"First, let's go back to the village and get some supplies." The two of them headed back into the village. The fires had stopped and there were just smoldering ruins where their houses had once been.

Jack went to the remains of his front door and dropped to his knees sobbing. "I am sorry, Mother. I should have saved you and I will find Elizabeth, I promise."

He got to his feet and went to meet Edward. After an hour of searching they had gathered enough food for a one way trip to Portsmouth.

"Well, let's go," said Edward. "I have said my goodbyes."

"Me too," replied Jack and with that the two of them set off.

They headed through the forest until they reached the road.

"So which way?" asked Edward.

"This way," replied Jack, pointing to the west.

"How do you know?" asked Edward. Jack pointed to a sign pointing down the road with Portsmouth written on it. Edward smirked and the two of them set of down the road chatting about better times from their childhood. After two hours of walking the two stopped to rest; they drank some water and then got up and continued walking.

As the sun was rising they arrived in Portsmouth. They immediately headed to the guard's post.

"Hold up there! What's the rush?" a guard said, putting out his hand.

"Please, you must help. Our village was raided by pirates," said Jack.

"This is very serious; wait here," the guard replied and went in to the building. A couple of minutes later he returned followed by ten others and an officer.

"Which way is your village?" asked the officer. Jack pointed to the west.

"All right you wait here, you two look exhausted, go to the inn and wait for us to return."

"Yes, sir," replied Jack. He and Edward headed off to the inn as the soldiers marched off down the road. The two young men entered the inn and found a table in the corner and took a seat, pulling out the food they had packed.

"It's not much but it's good," said Jack and he shared out the food between them. Jack beckoned over a waitress. "We need a room with two beds please," he said.

"It's on the house, word of what happened travels fast. I'm sorry about what happened," replied the waitress.

"Thank you for your kindness," said Jack. After the two of them had finished eating they just sat and talked for what seemed like hours. Then tiredness took them so they retired to the room.

***

Jack was the first to wake. He sat up looking around. Edward was sound asleep. Jack felt sad; the last time he had slept in a bed his mother was alive and he knew where his sister was. Sunlight was creeping in under the curtains. Jack woke Edward and the two of them left the room and went out to see what was going on.

When they entered the main room of the inn, the officer was standing there, his face solemn. "We saw your village, the destruction and...." he paused, wiping a tear from his eye, "bodies. We also found footprints leading towards the shore to the south. It looks like when they landed they went into the forest to hide before the attack. I'm sorry for your losses. The navy has been told and has dispatched a ship to try and find where they went."

"Any sign of my sister?" Jack interrupted.

"Your sister?"

"Yes. She was taken in the attack. I tried to stop them but I was beaten by their leader."

"That was brave of you to fight. Both of you would have made your families proud." The officer looked and spotted the bandage round Jack's face, "Did the pirate leader do that to you in combat?" he asked.

"No, after he knocked me down. I wounded him and then in rage he did this to me and told me I would see him again" Jack replied.

"Can I see it?" said the officer.

"Yes," replied Jack and turned his face. Edward carefully unwrapped the bandages revealing an ugly wound.

"You two need to come with me now." And with that the officer helped Edward cover up Jack's wound.

"We can't let anyone see this yet."

"Why?" asked Edward.

"We will talk at the headquarters." Then he turned and led the way to the headquarters. Jack and Edward followed. They entered headquarters, the officer came to attention and saluted another officer. "Sergeant William Boliton reporting, Sir."

The other officer returned the salute. "What are these two doing here, Sargent?"

"Major, these are the only survivors from the pirate attack, sir."

"Why does this warrant bringing them to the commander, Sargent?"

"The wound on the boy's face sir... It seems like you know who was behind the attack... This brave young lad fought him and wounded him, sir!"

"Really? That is worrying: he hasn't been seen outside the Caribbean before, and he certainly hasn't attacked any villages this far away... Very well, Sargent; good work."

"Thank you, sir." The officer opened the door and lead the way in to the commander's room, standing to attention and saluting. "Sir. Sergeant Boliton has brought witnesses from the attack from what I have been told it looks to be the work of the pirate known as Red Beard."

"Red Beard!" gasped the Commander, returning the salute. "Where's the evidence of this, Major?"

"Present your evidence, Sergeant."

"Yes, Sir. All right Son, show the wound on your face."
"Very well" replied Jack, "Can you help me please Edward?"

"Of course, Jack" and with that Edward began carefully removing the bandage from Jack's face revealing the nasty upside-down-triangle shaped wound. The Commander rose to his feet and walked up to Jack and carefully moved his head to the left to look at the wound.

"Sergeant."

"Yes, sir."

"Take this young man to the hospital and get this looked at. Last thing we want is for an infection to take hold."

"Yes, sir. All right, boys, you follow me."

"Wait," said Jack. "Please, sir, I want to find the man responsible for this as he also killed my mother and took my sister."

"Get that looked at first, then we can talk."

"Thank you, sir." And with that, Jack, escorted by Edward, followed the sergeant down the corridor.

The hospital wasn't far from the headquarters. Jack sat on a bed while the doctor looked at the wound. "Nurse bring me something to clean this up."

"Yes, Doctor."

"What can be done?" asked Edward.

"Nothing much. We will clean it but it seems to have scabbed over nicely. I don't see any sign of infection; the speed and skill of the person who bandaged it helped."

"Thank you," said Edward looking very proud of himself.

"There we go, that looks better," said the nurse, after she had finished cleaning the wound.

Jack looked a little pale – the cleaning had not been pain-free but he was glad it didn't look like a butcher had been at his face anymore!

"Thank you," he said, his voice trembling a bit as he didn't feel great. "Now can I go and talk to the Commander, please?"

"After you drink this," replied the doctor, handing Jack a cup of water. Jack drank the water then he and Edward followed the sergeant back to the Commander's room.

"Sir, I would like to join the navy in order to find this Red Beard," said Jack, standing up tall.

"How old are you?" replied the Commander.

"I am sixteen, sir."

"Hmm." The Commander paused, thinking. "Well, you're too old to be a powder lad but not old enough for a normal seaman, but under the circumstances I am going to put you under the command of Captain William Button. He is being tasked to go to the Caribbean and find Red Beard. Since you have your own sword and pistol and have already fought Red Beard, I am appointing you the midshipman."

"Thank you, sir." Jack struck a salute; the Commander saluted back.

"Sign here." The Commander produced a piece of paper and a quill. Jack signed quickly. "You are now officially part of his Majesty's Royal Navy. Report to the HMS *Revenge* at the docks."

"Yes, sir. Well I guess this is goodbye, Edward." Jack looked sad.

"Sir, is there any way for me to join my friend?" said Edward, turning to the commander.

"Well, we are a few soldiers short for the ship."

"I'll do it. I would like to be a marine, Sir." Edward enthusiastically stood to attention.

"It usually would require training, but this situation is unusual so we will get you trained on the ship on the way." The Commander got out another piece of paper and began writing. "Give this to Major James Woodwick, aboard the *Revenge*. He will make you officially a Marine Solider."

Edward took the paper. "Thank you, Sir. Looks like it's not goodbye after all." The two of them marched off towards the docks.

Chapter 9

The docks were alive with activity; ships being loaded and unloaded; women waiting for the sailors to come ashore; the sounds of people calling to each other, and even animal calls filled the air. Edward took it all in, having never seen anything like this before. Jack had been here before, so was less taken back. They searched for the *Revenge*. They found her pretty quickly, the soldiers posted at the boarding ramp giving away that this was a Royal Navy vessel. The *Revenge* was beautiful; a seventy gun frigate. Her hull looked the same as when Jack and his father had watched her launch. It brought back good memories. Jack and Edward approached the ramp.

"Halt!" said one of the guards in a stern tone of voice, pointing his weapon at the two of them; his red coat bright in the sun. "What business do you have approaching his majesty's ship?"

"I am midshipman Jack Leighton, I am here to see the captain," Jack said proudly, producing his papers.

"And I am Edward Rosley. I am to report to the major at once," and he also produced his papers.

"Very well," the soldier stopped pointing his weapon at them and Jack called out, "Permission to come aboard?"

"Permission granted," came a reply from the deck. The soldiers stood to attention and saluted. Jack and Edward returned the salute as they passed. Walking up the ramp they could feel the gentle sway and bobbing of the ship in the calm waters of the docks. Upon walking onto the deck they were approached by an officer in a red coat. This was the major, distinguished by the golden chevrons on his shoulders.

"Here are my papers, sir," said Edward, handing the major the paper.

The major unraveled it. Reading quickly he said, "Hmm, I am sorry for your loss, both of you."

"Thank you, sir," Jack and Edward replied.

"Well, it's good to have another soldier onboard. I thought we were going to be really short-handed. I will have you trained up in no time, Private."

"Yes, sir," Edward came to attention and saluted.

The major returned the salute. "Follow me. We'll get you your uniform and weapon." He turned and marched off with Edward following down the ramp.

Jack felt really alone for the first time since the village, when he heard footsteps behind him. Jack spun around towards the wheel and saw a man coming down the stairs. He was tall, dressed in dark blue with a hat in a dome shape. Jack could see the sun glinting off the medal on his chest. Jack quickly composed himself and stood to attention and struck a salute. The man stood returned the salute.

"Who are you?" he asked in a soft gentle voice.

"I am midshipman Jack, I have been assigned to this ship, sir."

"Well, it's a pleasure to meet you, Jack. Your papers please." Jack handed his paper rolled up to the man who he knew was Captain William Button. The captain read over the paper, his face changing the more he read. After he had finished reading he said, "I'm sorry for your loss, especially to this man."

"Thank you, sir." Jack could feel a wave of sadness and anger come over him as thoughts of what happened in the village came flooding back but he quickly hid it from his face.

"It's all right to feel angry and saddened by what has happened but don't let it consume you."

"Yes, sir." Jack felt a lot better. The captain was kind and made him feel at ease.

"Now go and get yourself a uniform befitting of a midshipman aboard my ship."

"Where do I go sir?"

"The tailor's is opposite the ship."

"Thank you, sir" and with that Jack saluted, turned and went down the ramp and into the tailors.

***

It took a few days for the uniforms to be ready and in that time Jack and Edward had been familiarizing themselves with the ship and life onboard. They picked up their uniforms, Jack's a dark blue and Edward's a bright red. After they were dressed in their uniforms they were ready to depart. The boarding ramp was removed,

The anchor was raised. Jack stood by the wheel with the captain; the captain had taken an instant liking to Jack and had been teaching him map-reading whilst he had been waiting for his uniform. The wind was good and the sails billowed out. The ship started to move.

"Sir, may I ask where are we going?"

"Yes, we are to go to Port Royal in the Caribbean; there we will begin our patrol."

"Thank you, sir."

***

It was many months at sea before they reached Port Royal. The first thing Jack noticed was the heat; Port Royal was as busy as Portsmouth with people coming and going. Jack had been put in charge of the sails.

"Reel in the main sail," shouted Jack. Men started clambering up the rigging, pulling ropes. Slowly, the sails began to rise. "Come on put your backs into it!" The sound of grunting echoed round the deck as the men worked feverishly to get the ship into port. It took about an hour to fully dock the ship and get supplies moving.

"Midshipman, accompany me to the admiral's headquarters to announce our arrival."

"Yes, sir," replied Jack. Edward and four other soldiers including the major escorted them.

***

Jack and Captain Button entered the admiral's room while the soldiers stood guard. Captain Button had his hat under his arm as they approached. "Sir Captain Button of the HMS *Revenge* reporting for duty."

"Good. I had been expecting your arrival for several days."

"Bad wind, sir."

"Well you're here now – what have you to report from England?"

"Sir, pirates attacked a village; killed everyone in it except two. This young officer is one of them." He gestured towards Jack. "The wound on his face and from witness accounts it looks to be the work of Red Beard."

"Red Beard!" The admiral's voice changed to that of shock and worry.

"That's who my ship has been deployed to hunt and bring to justice."

"Indeed. But I have more important use for you and your ship at this present time: escorting some merchants to the colonies. Other pirates and privateers have thought that the king's supplies are fair game. I need you to teach them otherwise."

"Sir, I have my orders."

"Yes, but you are now under my command. You can follow up on Red Beard after. Dismissed."

Jack's face had changed to that of anger. Captain Button saw this and just gently shook his head. The two of them returned to the ship.

"We will find Red Beard, Jack. I promise you."

"Sir, but the admiral..."

"The admiral is a fool. He is only doing this because he probably has a deal with the blighter, being out here for so long, and being looked over time and time again for the Channel Fleet. Now, do you trust me?"

"Yes, sir, always, sir."

"Good. Then let's get going."

Chapter 10

Unfortunately the admiral's tasks took up four long years. It was Jack's twentieth birthday and his frustration and anger at not being able to hunt for Red Beard had almost driven him to murder. At one point he almost drew his pistol on the admiral when Red Beard's ship had been spotted. Instead of pursuing Red Beard, the *Revenge* was ordered on another pointless escort mission. If it hadn't been for Captain Button he would have killed the admiral. Captain Button had almost become like a father to Jack, and in the years under his command, Jack had achieved the rank of Lieutenant Commander. It wasn't just Jack who had been promoted, Captain Button had been given the rank of Commodore. The years of pointless tasks had its upsides.

"Happy birthday, Jack" said Edward who had also been promoted to a sergeant and become a very capable soldier.

"Thank you," replied Jack. "I know I am meant to be more formal; Lieutenant Commander."

"Don't be silly, Edward. You are my best and oldest friend, besides, no-one's around."

Edward smiled looking up. "It's a nice night."

Jack looked up at the clear night sky "Yes, it is".

Then came a commotion from the docks; the two of them raced over to the railing and looked down towards the docks. The sound of musket fire rang out.

"Halt, murderer!" a solider shouted pointing at a man who was running down the docks his hands covered in blood. "Stop that man, he murdered the admiral!"

Edward grabbed his musket and took aim. "This is your last chance to stop!" he shouted. The man stopped and drew a pistol. Edward pulled the trigger but nothing happened.

"Damn! Misfire!" he exclaimed, then he looked and saw the man aiming at him. Edward jumped as a pistol shot rang out. He looked down expecting to see blood but there was none then he looked back at the man who was now on the floor in a pool of blood, a hole in his chest. Edward then looked round at Jack who was putting away his pistol, a solemn look on his face. Two guards came running up and looked at the body.

"He was a pirate, wasn't he?" called Jack.

One of the guards checked the man over. "Yes, sir." Then he pulled out a piece of paper from the man's pocket.

"Soldier, what is that?"

"Seems to be a map, sir." Jack walked down the ramp. "Let me see."

"Yes, sir."

Jack examined the drawings. "These are our trade routes." Jack then saw a marking at the bottom of the paper. "The inverted triangle!" he whispered, touching his scar.

"Sir?"

"Nothing. Soldier, get this body out of here, I must report to the commodore."

"Yes, sir."

Jack then turned and marched quickly up the ramp. The noise had woken most of the ship; Commodore Button came out of his quarters. "What is going on out here?"

"Sir, The Admiral has been murdered," Jack said.
"Murdered?"

"Yes, sir. The man who did it was killed trying to flee. He was carrying this on his person." Jack handed over the map.

"Hmmm." Commodore Button studied the map, his face changing as he saw the mark at the bottom. "Is that..."

"Yes, sir. Red Beard's mark. It does seem The Admiral was working with the pirates by choice, or by fear. We will never know."

"Indeed. But now we know Red Beard is close, we can start searching immediately."

***

The next morning at the crack of dawn, the *Revenge* set sail.

"We will head west,"

"Sir?" This was the first time Jack had felt like his old self again; finally they were looking for Red Beard. "Sergeant, a word." Jack called out.

Edward turned and looked and saw Jack walking down the steps towards him. "Yes, sir."

"Are you all right?" Jack said in a hushed tone.

"What do you mean, sir?"

"You know what I mean. We are finally hunting Red Beard."

"Yes, and yes it does make me think of that night in the village; the screams; the blood; my first kill."

"Me too. The pain of my face and the fact I lost my sister."

"You will find her, Jack, I know you will."

"Thank you, my friend." The two exchanged a look; it was a look that only best friends would understand, a look that said things will be all right. "Very good Sergeant, continue with your weapon cleaning."

"Yes, sir."

Jack returned to the bridge.

"Everything all right Lieutenant Commander?"

"Yes, sir."

After a day of sailing the *Revenge* reached a known pirate-raiding route.

"Keep your eyes open men," called The Commodore.

A light mist was around the ship and the wind was calm. The ship was only moving a couple of knots, the waves, gently lapping up against the hull.

"Smoke off the port bow!" shouted the lookout, pointing.

"Full sail, come about, head for the smoke."

"Aye, aye, sir," The Helmsman replied.

As the *Revenge* approached, the smoke from a burning ship loomed into view.

"Reel in the main sail!" Jack shouted. "Look out for survivors."

"Yes, sir." The Commodore was looking at the burning ship. "That's the *Nottingham*; she was due in port two days ago. God help the men on board – any sign of survivors?"

"No, sir," came the reply.

"It's him," said Jack, his voiced laced with anger.

"Easy, Jack," replied a calm Commodore.

"Enemy ship to starboard," called the lookout.

"Action stations, roll out the guns," shouted The Commodore. One of the men started ringing the bell, men were scrambling to their stations. Edward and the other soldiers ran to the starboard railing and readied their weapons. The enemy ship was closing in from the right side.

"Hard to starboard, bring us along-side." shouted The Commodore at The Helmsmen, his voice only just being heard over the commotion of soldiers and men running about the deck. Jack ran up to the commodore.

"Sir, it's a brig, no more than thirty guns and sixteen crew, that is not the ship that destroyed the Nottingham.

"Very good, Lieutenant Commander."

"Thank you, sir".

Jack walked to the railing and looked over the deck; the men were in position. The guns were being loaded and pulled in to position. The gun ports opened as each gun was ready. The ships were now parallel.

"Steady, steady," the commodore called to the men. You could cut the tension with a knife as the ships closed in on each other. The ships came alongside each other, the silence was broken only by the wind catching the sails and the sea lapping against the hull. Then all hell broke loose with the commodore shouting out, "Fire!"

The command every man onboard had been waiting for; the sound of hissing as the powder was lit, then thirty-five guns went off, almost in unison the same time the brigs guns fired the sound was deafening. Smoke filled the deck; splinters flew everywhere, iron balls from the enemy brig tore through the oak of the *Revenge's* hull. Men cried out in pain as splinters tore through their bodies, men were lying there with their guts hanging out where the splinters had ripped through their flesh. Jack was horrified at what he was seeing; it reminded him of that night in the village, but the brig was even worse.

Jack looked over at the brig, which was pretty much devoid of life after the first broadside. Only a couple of wounded pirates remained. Blood stained the entire deck of the enemy ship; bodies were everywhere, some were missing arms and legs. One had been hit by a cannon ball and just exploded. One pirate remained uninjured and he was determined to make a fight of it. Edward put him down with his first shot; his first kill as a soldier.

The sounds and smells of battle lingered... Jack threw up over the side.

"It's all right, it's natural; shows you're human," said Commodore Button, putting his hand on Jacks back, as Jack continued to throw up. Strangely, Edward was less affected, barely showing any emotion, he even looked like he enjoyed killing the pirate. Jack wiped his mouth and looked at his friend. Edward looked back but the look he gave made Jack uneasy; that wasn't the look of his friend.

"Torch the brig, then set course for port, we need repairs," said the commodore. Every man not injured went to their posts. The guns were retracted and the gun ports closed. The soldiers threw flaming torches onto the brigs' deck which caught and went up in flames. The flames grew as the *Revenge* set off for port.

Chapter 11

The return to port was quiet. After the ship docked, carpenters came aboard and started repairing the damage. The bodies were carried off. Jack and the commodore stood, hands behind their backs, watching. The men who had died from infection were on the way back to port. The men killed outright had been buried at sea. Jack had a feeling in his stomach that these men who had died and those wounded trying to bring Red Beard to justice were just the beginning. Many more would perish in pursuit of the man who brought Jack and Edward so much pain and suffering.

"It's good you feel sad for these men," said the commodore.

Jack looked at him. "How did you know, sir?"

The Commodore let out a chuckle. "We have been on this ship together for over four years. I know you. Your compassion is good. Don't let your anger at Red Beard consume you. There is life after Red Beard."

"Thank you, sir. I won't"

"Just remember that when you come face to face with Red Beard."

"I will, sir," Jack replied, even though he knew it wouldn't be as easy as that.

Jack went ashore and found a local tavern. When he went inside he found Edward gulping down a pint of ale. Jack ordered one himself, then went over and sat with his friend.

"What are you doing here, Edward?" Jack whispered to his friend.

"Drinking." replied Edward, barely looking at Jack.

"You didn't get permission to leave the ship."

"What of it?"

"I'm your friend but I am also an officer of His Majesty's Navy, you can get in a lot of trouble for leaving without permission."

"I don't care."

"What has happened to you?"

"Nothing. Now leave me alone."

"Fine. If that's the way you want it." Jack stood up and finished his drink. "Soldier, I expect you back on the ship in ten minutes."

Edward just looked at Jack. The look on his face made Jack uneasy. Then he looked back and beckoned for another drink. Jack felt an anger build up inside him; he turned and stormed out of the tavern. As he was heading back to the ship he overheard two pirates talking down an ally.

"That's right, two plump, ripe merchants loaded to the brim with cargo."

"We better go back, tell the captain."

Jack quickly rushed to the ship he went up to The Major. "Sir, Sergeant has left the ship without permission and is now getting drunk down at the tavern. Take some men and bring him back."

"Yes, sir," replied the major as he waved over two soldiers. They headed off towards the tavern. Jack went and knocked at the commodore's quarters.

"Come," came a voice. Jack opened the door, removing his hat and stood in front of the commodore's desk. The commodore was sitting writing something. Jack saluted. the commodore looked up.

"What is it, commander?"

"Sir, I just overheard two pirates planning an attack on two merchant ships."

"Two ships traveling together?"

"Yes, sir, that's how it sounded."

"Hmm, that must be the *Devon* and the *Liverpool*; they are due into port in three days." He looked at another piece of paper. "Oh dear, they seem to be laden with spices and gold; we must go and protect them. Tell the men to prepare the ship."

"Yes, sir. Oh, um… one more thing, sir,"

"Yes?"

"Sergeant left the ship without permission and was found getting drunk. I sent the major to bring him back. What should be the punishment?"

"He is your friend is he not?"

"He used to be, now I'm seeing a change in him."

"I see. Put him in the brig for seven days."

"Yes, sir." Jack then turned and left. When outside, he took a deep breath. He wanted to help Edward but didn't know how.

***

The carpenters worked flat out through the night to fix as much as they could.

Jack watched as Edward was dragged onboard shouting, "You did this! You did this to me!"

Jack tried to ignore him but inside it hurt to see his friend like this. They dragged Edward to the brig.

"Took your time, Major."

"Sorry, sir. We had to find him."

"Find him?"

"Yes, sir. After the tavern he was wandering through the streets."

"Very well, Major. Good job for bringing him back in one piece. Continue with what you were doing."

"Yes, sir. Thank you, sir."

***

The ship was ready by first light. There was an almighty commotion on deck, men running about doing their duties: raising the anchor; prepping the sails and cleaning the guns. Soon they were under way.

"Head due west," Commodore Button called to the navigator.

"Yes, sir, due west, sir," came the reply. The navigator worked hard at the wheel and the ship came about.

"We will follow the trade route until we find the ships."

"Aye aye, sir."

The wind was good and the *Revenge* made great time. It would take at least a day and a half with good wind to meet up with the ships.

That night, the sea was calm and the wind was strong. Jack walked around the deck doing his nightly rounds. He could barely sleep more than a couple of hours at a time; every time he closed his eyes he had terrible nightmares about his mother, sister and Red Beard and that night when his whole world changed. He usually got to the screams before he woke, often in a cold sweat, so most nights he walked the deck looking at the stars and imagining his mother and father looking back at him. He looked out over the blank sea. Though teaming with life beneath the waves, on top it was dead. He longed to see his sister safe and well looking back, calling to him.

The next day the lookouts were on alert, as were the gunners and soldiers. Jack paid a visit to Edward in the brig. He looked in, then turned and as he was walking away Edward called out, "I am sorry, my friend."

Jack paused then as he walked away said, "I hope our friendship will survive this."

***

The sun was high in the sky. The commodore checked his watch. "Noon. We should have seen them by now."

Everything was silent. The wind had died down so the ship was just crawling along. The silence seemed to go on for an eternity then a call broke the silence: "Ship ahoy!" came from the lookout, pointing to the north.

"Action stations!" shouted the commodore.

"Sir, what is wrong?"

"The merchants would be coming from the south west."

The scramble that came afterwards was a sight to behold: the guns were reeled out and the men readied their weapons. The commodore was determined to be better than last time, the casualties still weighing heavily on his mind.

"Another ship behind!" the lookout called,

"What flag are they flying?"

"Black with an inverted triangle, sir."

Jack felt a lump in his throat. "What ships are they?" he called

"One corvette and one galleon," came the reply.

"Sir, neither of them are Red Beard's ship but they do belong to Red Beard."

"Yes. It seems he is better equipped than we thought, but how do you know that he's not onboard?"

"When I fought him, what I saw of his clothing and his weapons, his ship is probably a frigate or razee – he seems to like expensive things, things no other pirate would have."

"I see. That's a good train of thought and seeing as he has his own flag that would suggest he thinks of himself as an admiral. This could be very dangerous to the whole region."

The ships closed on each other, the *Revenge* hampered by the wind being against them. The pirate vessels had now gone side by side, no doubt planning to come either side of the *Revenge*.

"Jack, under no circumstance can this ship be taken, do you understand?"

Jack just nodded, surprised that the commodore had called him by his name rather than rank. The ships went alongside the *Revenge*, their sails were up.

"They plan to board us!" shouted Jack.

Then came the order to fire the guns on both sides. The *Revenge* thundered in to life! The galleon fired first, then the corvette. Jack watched as the soldiers on board were firing at pirates, swinging grappling hooks. Jack drew his sword and saw as the commodore did the same. The guns where firing as fast as they could be loaded; smoke covered the deck, the smell of gun powder heavy in the air. Boys were running up from below decks with more powder; splinters flew in all directions; injured men were carried down to the surgeon. Then thuds were heard as grappling hooks dug into the oak. The ropes behind them going from slack to taut as the pirates pulled their ships closer. The cannons kept firing, going from round shot to grape shot.

"Prepare to repel boarders!" shouted Jack. The first pirates swung on to the deck and a fierce melee broke out on the deck. Swords clashed, pistol shots were lost in the sounds of cannon fire, then the ramps were lowered from the pirate ships and on came a stream of angry, snarling pirates brandishing swords and knives. One made a beeline for Jack – their swords meet with a clang. Jack's form had improved ten-fold and after a couple of parries, Jack dispatched the pirate with a swift stab to the chest, his blade going straight through until the point was seen out the other side. When he pulled it out he noticed his hand was also covered in blood. He didn't know but his sword had pierced the man's heart. The battle continued for hours. The decks of all three ships littered with bodies. Blood ran off the decks and the sounds of battle had not died down. Jack had killed at least a dozen men. His clothes stained with blood and he had a cut on his arm from one of the fights. Then the pirate captain came into the battle. Jack saw him heading up to the wheel. Jack raced after him as he got to the top of the stairs. The captain from the covette stood in front of him then the two started fighting. Jack could see out of the corner of his eye as their swords were locked and they span around, The Commodore fighting the pirate captain from The Galleon. Then everything went into slow motion for Jack: he saw the pirate knock the commodore's sword from his hand.

"Noooo!" shouted Jack as the captain drove his sword through William Button's abdomen. Anger suddenly engulfed Jack. With a flick of his wrist he slashed the captain he was fighting across the chest, he dropped his sword, clutching his chest. Jack raised his foot and kicked him down the stairs, then Jack turned and charged at the other captain, his eyes laced with anger, as though he had just been possessed. As his sword met the captain's, a cheer went up from the deck. The rest of the men had beaten the pirates! Then the men on the deck looked up in horror as they watched Jack battle this pirate captain and they caught a glimpse of the commodore lying on the floor, blood dripping down the stairs. Jack's attacks were wild and aggressive, the sound of their swords clashing echoed around the deck as the cannons had stopped firing. Then the pirate captain swiped at Jack's head. Jack rolled and as he rolled he grabbed the commodore's sword in his left hand. Then he got back to his feet. The pirate came at him again, this time Jack used one sword to block the attack while using the other sword to slash across the pirate's stomach. As the pirate's sword dropped, Jack used the right handed sword and drove it through his stomach, followed quickly by the second one. Jack watched the life drain from the pirates face. Before the pirate captain's lifeless body had hit the floor, Jack had let go of his swords and rushed to the side of the commodore.

"Sir, sir, William," he said, almost in tears as he cradled his head. "Please, don't die."

The commodore opened his eyes, as a trickle of blood ran down the side of his mouth, he smiled. "You did well, Jack. The ship is yours now."

"No, sir, it's yours. You are going to be fine."

"No, Jack. I know I will not make it this time." He coughed as more blood came from his mouth. Jack had put his hands on the wound trying desperately to stop the bleeding. "I have survived injuries before but not like this. The only regret I have is I didn't have a son like you."

Jack tried to smile, tears streaming down his cheeks. "You're like a father to me."

"Thank you, Jack. My son." With that, William Button took his last breath.

Just as the rest of the crew got to the top of the stairs, the major came and put his hand on Jack's shoulder. "He's gone, sir."

Jack slumped back, covered in blood.

"He really did think of you like a son." The major then stood up. "Thank you, Major" Jack stood up and saluted and so did the rest of the crew.

The trip back to port was a sad one. No one really said much. The commodore's body was put in a barrel of brandy to preserve it for the trip back to England. The other men who had died were sewn up in their hammocks and lined up on the deck. There were at least thirty men and three powder boys.

Jack, now as the acting captain, stood and addressed the crew: "Men, you have fought well but we have lost many friends and comrades. Now, with the grace of God we commit them to the sea they fought so hard to protect. May they rest in peace."

Jack turned and saluted as one by one the bodies were cast in to the sea. After the last one, Jack went into the captain's quarters to change his blood-soaked clothes. There on the desk was the paper the commodore had been writing, folded in half and 'Jack' written on it. Jack picked it up, opened it and started reading. It read:

> *Jack, if you're reading this then I did not survive the battle we set out for. Before we left, I put in for your promotion to Captain. Congratulations, I can think of no one better to look after my ship. I knew from the day I met you, you would rise to greatness and over the years you became like the son I never had. I know you will find your sister, and please remember what I told you: don't let Red Beard consume you and don't give up on Edward.*
>
> *Yours sincerely, Commodore William A Button.*

Jack put the paper down feeling sad and proud at the same time. One thing was sure – he would find Red Beard.

Chapter 12

The trip back to port was solemn; the entire crew was feeling down and glum. Jack sat at the desk that once belonged to his mentor. He was trying to write a letter to accompany Commodore William Button's body back to England, but every time he started to write a wave of sadness came over him. He put down the quill and put his face in his hands. He kept thinking it was a trap the whole time and that if he had been faster he could have saved the commodore. A knock came at the door.

"Enter," Jack called, the door opened and in walked one of the crew. "Yes, what is it?"

"Sir, we have arrived at port."

"Good. Begin docking, I will be out shortly."

"Yes, sir." The crew member left. Jack had barely looked up at him during the whole conversation.

After the ship had docked Jack went to the brig.

"Open the door," he said to the guard.

"Yes, sir," the guard then turned unlocked and opened the door. Edward sat up.

"You are to return to you post immediately." Jack spoke in a very low tone.

"Yes, sir, I heard about the commodore. I am sorry; I know how close you were to him." Jack had already turned around and started walking away.

"Thank you, my friend."

Jack went up to the top deck and looked out over Port Royal. He then turned and called over to the two soldiers talking to each other by the railing. "You two, come with me."

The two soldiers both turned and looked over at him. "Yes, sir," they said, grabbing their weapons.

At the top of the ramp the major called out to Jack. "Sir, what about the commodore's body?"

"Prepare the men and bring the body up here, the ship taking him back to England will be here within the next two hours. I shall be back by then."

"Yes, Sir."

Jack and the soldiers travelled into town. As they passed the tavern, Jack heard the same voices he had heard before. Jack could just about make what was being said.

"Haha, dumb Navy types. Red Beard will reward us greatly for this."

"Reward us? He will kill us!"

"What do you mean?"

"The ship survived and both captains are dead."

"Yes but the commodore is..." Jack had heard enough and before the soldiers had time to stop him he was down the alley punching the pirate. The other tried to run but tripped over and when he looked up he was looking down the barrel of a musket: "You're under arrest." said the soldier. The other soldier however was trying to stop Jack who was now on top of the pirate. The soldier ran to the end of the ally; he looked round and saw two more soldiers patrolling.

"You two, I need help!" The two soldiers raced over. The three of them ran down the alley and saw Jack still punching a now unconscious pirate. The soldiers grabbed him and pulled him off the pirate. Jack struggled against them

"Sir, stop please."

"Drag them to the prison and get them to tell you where Red Beard is!" Jack shouted. "And I do not care how you get them to tell you. Just make them talk."

"Yes, Sir." The two soldiers holding Jack let go then went and dragged the unconscious pirate away, followed by the other pirate being led at gun point.

"Once they talk, come and tell me what they say, but do not return to the ship until they talk."

"Yes, sir."

"Come, sir, we must return to the ship and have your hands seen to before the commodore's body needs to be handed over." And with that, the two of them set off back to the ship.

***

Jack was being seen by the surgeon, his hands bruised and swollen.

"What have you been up to, sir?"

"I ran in to some pirates." Jack smiled awkwardly.

"Well, by the looks of your hands I wound not like to be the one fixing them up." The surgeon put cold, soaked bandages round Jack's hands. Jack winced in pain. "There, that will take the swelling down. It does not look like you have broken anything"

"Thank you."

"Anytime, sir. I just wish all the patients I have to see only had wounds like yours." Jack got up and left the surgeon's quarters.

Jack returned to the top deck where news of what had happened had already spread around the crew. Jack looked around and saw all the crew stand up and start clapping. The major approached him.

"What is going on?"

"They are happy to see you finally grieve, that you're just like them."

"I am an officer, I should not have done what I did."

"You could have killed him but you didn't. I think every man in your shoes would have done the same thing."

"Thank you." Jack then addressed the crew. "Thank you all, I know it is hard to lose a captain. I know it is even harder to lose a friend, but we will find the leader of these pirates and we will bring him to justice."

The whole crew let out a cheer. The crew lined the deck for the handing-over ceremony. They all struck a salute as the barrel containing The Commodore's body was taken off the ship. Jack, holding back tears, was the last one the barrel passed, Jack then felt a hand on his shoulder. He turned his head and looked – it was Edward. At last it seemed his friend was back to normal but Jack still had an uneasy feeling about him.

Along with taking the body back to England, the ship had also brought a new admiral to take over. The first thing he did was address Jack. "My deepest condolences. Commodore William Button was a good man, but now congratulations are in order. I know it's jumping a few ranks, but I need someone who knows the ship, her crew and these waters, so I am pleased to promote you to Captain and give you command of the *Revenge*."

"Thank you, sir."

"I have only one order for you and your ship: find Red Beard and bring him here, he has a date with the gallows that's long overdue."

"Yes, sir." Jack felt a happiness inside as finally he had direct orders to find Red Beard. After the admiral had left, the major approached Jack.

"Your orders, Captain," he said, smiling. "Send a message to the tailors requesting a new captain's uniform."

"Yes, sir. Anything else, sir?"

"Yes. We are taking the ship to sea immediately."

"Yes, sir." The major then sent a runner with the message while the ship was being readied. Soon the *Revenge* was underway. Jack stood proudly on the bridge watching as his men worked seamlessly climbing up and down the rigging, swabbing the decks and making sure the guns were clean and ready for action.

***

It took a day of sailing with favorable winds to reach the trade routes often known to be frequented by pirates.
"Anything to report?" Jack called through cupped hands to the lookout in the crow's nest.

"Nothing yet, sir," came the reply.

Hours passed and still nothing until, "Wreckage off the port bow!" called the lookout,

"Come about and dip the main sail – keep a look out for survivors!" shouted Jack.

Men scrambled to their posts. The main sail was folded up and men on the deck raced to the side looking down for survivors, but only seeing jagged and broken pieces of timber. Jack looked on, as they got closer to the source of the wreckage, bigger and bigger pieces could be seen; a mast floated by. Jack leant forward and squinted.

Pointing, he shouted, "There's a survivor!"

The men lowered down over the side and pulled the survivor from the water. Jack raced down the stairs as the survivor was brought on board. "Keep looking for more survivors!"

Jack then heard coughing, followed by a low voice, "There are none."

Jack pushed through the men and there on the deck was a young woman.

"What do you mean?" he said, crouching at her side.

"They were all killed," said the woman before passing out.

"Get her to the surgeon now. Sergeant, you are to accompany her," Jack ordered and nodded at Edward who was happy to have Jack trust him with an order again. Jack ordered the ship to keep searching, but after three hours of searching they found nothing so Jack ordered the ship to keep heading along the trade route; he was determined to find the pirates responsible for the destruction of the ship.

Chapter 13

As the *Revenge* continued on course, Jack took some time to go down to the surgeon's quarters and check on the woman survivor.

"How is she?" he asked.

"She is conscious and has been asking for the captain,"

"Well, I better not keep her waiting." Jack's tone was slightly aggressive.

"Is there something wrong, Captain?"

"No, nothing." Jack then entered the room and saw the woman lying on the floor under a blanket, her head resting on a rolled up soldier's jacket. Jack approached. The woman sat up slowly. Jack felt a strange feeling come over him as he looked into her green eyes. He quickly quashed it remembering what must be done. The woman brushed her long, amber hair from her face.

"Are you the captain?"

Jack stood up straight and replied, "Yes, madam, Captain Jack Leighton at your service. What is your name?"

"My name is Daisy Maylor. Where am I?"

"You are onboard His Majestie's ship, the *Revenge*. We pulled you from a ship wreckage."

"Oh, I see."

"You don't seem too shocked?"

"No, I am. It is just a lot to take in."

Daisy then stood up. She was wearing boots, trousers and a white frock with a necklace. Jack looked at the necklace but Daisy quickly hid it in her top. She also had a jacket that was laid neatly on the floor with a long bulge in the centre, but neither Jack nor the surgeon had noticed. Jack was walking away then he looked back at her. "When you're feeling better we should talk more in my quarters."

Daisy looked at him, a soft look in her eyes. "Yes, Jack."

Jack just stared at her. "That's Captain, until I can be sure of your intentions."

Daisy just smiled cheekily at him, Jack turned then walked out.

"What is wrong with him?" Daisy said to the Surgeon.

"Pirates have taken a lot from him."

"How much?" Daisy replied, a look of concern on her face.

"I should not tell you, it is not my place." The surgeon went to turn away but Daisy put her hand on his shoulder.

"Please tell me."

The Surgeon sighed. "All right I will tell you. The one called Red Beard killed his mother and took his sister when he was sixteen. Recently, pirates from his fleet killed his mentor Commodore William Button. He has been hunting Red Beard for over five years." Daisy wiped a tear from her eye. "But please do not tell the Captain I told you."

"I won't." Daisy then went and laid back down.

Later that day Jack was sitting in his quarters thinking about Daisy. The feelings he was feeling were strange and he didn't understand what to do. Then he shook his head and said to himself, "No. I must not let my feelings cloud my vision of what I must do..." his train of thought was interrupted by a knock at the door. "Enter."

The door opened and Jack looked as Daisy walked in.

"Please take a seat," he said as he guided her to the chair. Daisy sat down. Just as they were about to start talking another knock came at the door. "Yes, what is it?"

The major opened the door. "Sir, should we head back to port?"

"Why?"

"Sir, the survivor – should we not bring her to port and report to the admiral?"

Jack's eyes narrowed a look of anger flashed across his face. "Absolutely not. We will continue the patrol and find those pirates"

"But, sir…"

Jack slammed both hands on his desk and stood up. "But nothing! You have your orders, major," he bellowed.

"Yes, sir," and with that the Major quickly left.

Jack sat back down. He looked at Daisy, still trying to be stern, but gazing into her eyes his demeanor started to soften. "Now, Miss Maylor."

"Daisy, please."

"All right, Daisy. What were you doing on that ship?"

Daisy stayed silent, looking around. Jack continued to ask questions but Daisy didn't answer any of them. Jack became increasingly frustrated but he remembered what Commodore Button had told him: *Don't let Red Beard consume you.* Jack just said, "That's all I wanted to ask. You can sleep in my quarters until we dock in a few weeks."

Daisy was wary. "But where will you sleep?"

"I don't most of the time and when I do I stay on deck and look at the stars."

"Thank you."

"One last thing," he said.

"Yes?"

"How old are you?"

Daisy smiled. "I just turned twenty"

"Thank you."

That night, Jack was wandering the deck, as usual, listening to the waves lap up against the ship's hull and feeling the cool breeze on his face. He didn't see Daisy open the door and look at him. She closed the door just as Jack turned to come back.

Jack closed his eyes but all he could see was the people he had lost; the screaming and smell of death. When he opened his eyes the sun was just rising, he saw Daisy standing at the railing watching the sun come up.

Jack walked up to her. "It is going to be a beautiful day."

Daisy turned her head and looked at him. "I hope so."

That day was quiet; not much happened except a crew member that fell head-first into a barrel. It took an hour to get him out.

***

The days went by and Jack and Daisy grew closer and closer. One evening the two were standing together by the railing.

Daisy asked, "Captain..."

"Please, call me, Jack."

"All right, Jack. Why are you so determined to find these pirates?" She already knew the answer but wanted Jack to tell her.

Jack's face showed his sadness; he looked down and said, "This pirate's men killed my mother, my mentor and took my sister."

"Don't forget your best friend's parents, or had you forgotten about me?" chimed in Edward, who was patrolling the deck and came over.

"Of course I did not forget you, but that does not excuse you from addressing me properly!"

"Yes, Captain," Edward said sarcastically.

Jack sighed. "Oh, not this again. Please excuse me, Daisy." Daisy just smiled and nodded, Jack walked over to Edward, "What is your problem? We are still hunting for Red Beard are we not?"

"Yes, but..."

"But what?"

"You're spending the days with her!"

"What about Daisy?"

"You're going soft!"

"How dare you! So what, I can't be happy and still find Red Beard?" Edward just stormed off. "Don't you dare just walk away from me, Sergeant!"

Edward just waved his hand and kept walking. Jack was about to go after him but Daisy stopped him. Just as Jack was about to say something Daisy kissed him.

"What was that?" she asked.

"He has been this way for months, I should really go after him."

"No, just stay here with me and finish telling me about these pirates."

"Well, it is just one really – their leader, the one known as Red Beard."

"Red Beard!" Daisy's voice trembled saying the name.

"You know the name?" Jack asked,

"Just through stories and hearsay."

"All right." Jack smiled at her.

"He was also the one who gave me this." Jack turned his face to show the scar. Daisy put her hand on it. Jack closed his eyes, her warm hand feeling good on his cheek. He reached up and put his hand on hers and then the two embraced, holding each other while looking out over the sea, the sun's light slowly creeping towards them.

"Well I had better be going to my post; the rest of the crew will be up soon." Jack said after half an hour.

Daisy brushed her hair from her face. "See you soon" she said.

Jack turned and waved as he walked.

Chapter 14

Everything was silent that day until, "Ship dead ahead!" broke the silence.

"What colours is she flying?" called Jack.

"It's..." the lookout squinted until the flag came into focus. "Black with a white skull."

"Pirates! Man your action stations!" shouted Jack. The crew, now well drilled in what to do, got to their stations. The guns were rolled out and loaded faster than they had ever been. Jack was walking on the main deck when he saw the door to his quarters open and Daisy standing there.

Jack raced up to her. "Stay inside and don't come out till I tell you!"

"But..."

Jack kissed her. "No buts." Then he turned. As she closed the door he brought out his spyglass and looked.

"It is a galleon," he called to the crew. "Be prepared they may try to board," he added. The soldiers loaded there weapons and the sharpshooters took their place in the rigging. The winds were good and soon the *Revenge* was alongside the enemy ship.

"Fire!" shouted Jack, drawing his sword. The guns fired. The noise was deafening as the two ships engaged each other. Broadside after broadside were fired. Wooden splinters flew through the air, splinters impaling men that were in their way; screams of the wounded echoed round the deck. The soldiers fired. The small pops of their guns drowned out by the cannon fire. Jack watched in horror as men fell all around. He raced over to the railings. "They are preparing to board us! Get ready to defend yourselves!"

Swords were passed among the crew, the cannons now loaded with grapeshot, fired and killed many pirates with every blast but soon the pirates were on board. The cannons in the lower decks kept firing, the melee that followed was unlike any before. Jack was fighting down on the deck when he heard Edward cry out in pain. He looked over and saw his friend clutching his arm. He kept fighting using his sword as he couldn't hold his musket anymore. He pushed the pirate back but just as he was about to press the advantage, a shot rang out. Edward stumbled back, clutching his abdomen. The pirate's pistol still smoking, Jack began racing over to his friend. He heard a crash and Daisy scream. He stopped. The pirate was baring down on Edward and he looked at his friend. Pulling his pistol, Jack took aim and fired the shot. Luckily it flew straight and true hitting the pirate in the back of the head! He was dead before he hit the floor. Edward watched as Jack turned and raced towards his quarters. Edward slumped down the railing. Jack entered his quarters and saw two pirates towering over Daisy.

"Leave her alone!" he snarled at them.

One spun around, swords drawn. The first one charged at him. Jack dispatched him quickly with a swift thrust to the chest. The other was still standing over Daisy. Jack walked up behind him. "Drop your weapon or you will die where you stand." The pirate threw down his sword. "Turn around," Jack said. The pirate complied, turning around, his hands above his head.

"Please, sir, don't kill me," he said, trembling. Jack stayed silent. The major came in behind him.

"Sir, the rest of the pirates have surrendered."

"How is Edward? I mean sargent?"

"He is all right. The ball didn't hit anything vital, the surgeon said. He will recover, he just needs rest."

"Good. Set course for port and take the prisoners to the brig and clap them in irons."

"Yes, sir." The major marched the pirate out of the quarters.

Jack turned to Daisy. "Are you all right?"

She smiled at him. "Yes, thank you. If you had not come when you did who knows what they might have done."

Jack felt uneasy. "That pirate had ample time to kill you, why didn't he?"

"He looked scared. Maybe he was new."

"Hmm… Maybe." Jack didn't believe her but was too tired to question her.

***

The trip back was quiet. The men went about their duties. The dead were put in to the sea, the wounded were cared for. Some limbs had to be amputated. Jack checked on Edward only to find him still unconscious. The crew repaired what they could but the damage was significant and required more men and materials to fully fix. Upon returning to port, the wounded, including Edward, were transported to the shore hospital and the prisoners taken to jail.

Jack followed a few days later, determined to find answers. He entered the jail and found the soldier who he had left in charge of the pirates.

"Sir."

"Any word from the ones we brought in?"

"I'm afraid not. They would not talk and were hanged about a week ago."

"Hanged? I wanted answers from them!"

"The judge said they must pay for their crimes and sentenced them to death. I am sorry, sir."

"It's not your fault. You did your duty. Well, take a day of rest then return to the ship."

"Yes, sir, thank you sir." And with that, the soldier left.

Jack found the pirate he had personally captured. "I want to speak to that one on his own," he said to the head jailer.

"Very well, sir." The jailer took the pirate to a separate cell. Jack followed.

The pirate immediately started pleading with him. "Please, sir, spare me!"

"Tell me why you didn't kill the young woman in the cabin."

"Err... I froze. I was thinking of different things to do with her."

Jack slapped him across the face. "Liar! Tell me why you didn't kill her, you had ample time."

"My life would have been forfeited in a way no man would care to think about if I had killed her."

Jack grabbed him by the collar. "Why?"

"Because she is Red Beard's daughter."

Jack let go, stepping back in shock. "You lie!"

"I have no reason to, sir."

Jack turned and walked out still in disbelief at what he had been told. "He told me the truth. Let the judge know this," Jack said to the jailer.

"Yes, sir."

Jack left the jail and headed for the ship determined to get the truth from Daisy.

He was half way there when Edward came up to him. "You left me bleeding to death, for her!" he shouted.

"I don't need this now Edward," Jack said. He went to carry on walking when Edward grabbed him. Jack span around. "What are you doing out of the hospital?"

"Oh, now you care. What about on the deck? What if you had missed?"

Jack looked down, thinking.

"I knew it. You would have left me to die for that whore!"

Jack punched Edward. "Don't you dare refer to Daisy that way!"

Edward held his jaw. Jack turned and started walking off.

"I will see you again, my old friend," Edward shouted to him. Jack didn't even stop, nor did he look back. Jack stormed up the ramp. The ship looked a lot better; the carpenters had done a great job in such a small amount of time; but Jack didn't have time to admire the craftsmanship.

The major met him on the deck, having to nearly run to keep up with him. "Sir..."

"Is Daisy in my quarters?"

"Yes, sir, why?"

"I need to talk to her I am not to be disturbed."

"Yes, sir."

Jack didn't even knock, he just burst through the door. Daisy saw the fury on Jack's face.

"Why didn't you tell me!" he bellowed.

"Tell you what?" she replied.

"That you're Red Beard's daughter!"

Daisy started to cry. "I... I'm nothing like him."

"Where is my sister?" Daisy continued to cry. "Don't let my love for you..."

"You love me?" Daisy stopped crying.

"Yes. I do," said Jack, his voice calming.

"I love you, too," she said, approaching Jack. She put her hands round his waist.

"Why were you on that ship?" Jack asked calmly.

"I wasn't. I was dumped in the wreckage when I wouldn't kill the captain."

"You were dumped?"

"Yes. My own father dumped me off, just for not being a killer."

"You could have told me."

Daisy put her head on Jack's chest. "I wanted to but I thought you would think of me like you think of him."

"Never."

Daisy lifted her head and the two of them kissed passionately. Daisy started to undo the buttons on Jack's coat as he started to undo her top. Jack lifted her into his arms and carried her to the bed.

Chapter 15

Jack was asleep with Daisy, her head on his chest. Jack, for once, had a smile on his face. His dreams not full of death and screaming, but finally of what his life might be after this was all over. But it was short-lived as cannon balls ripped through the ship, splinters barley missing the two of them.

Jack dove across to protect Daisy. "Are you all right?" he asked, out of breath.

"Yes, yes. I'm fine, what's going on?"

"I don't know."

They heard a commotion outside, the sounds of gun fire and swords clashing. Jack grabbed his undergarment, just about managing to pull it on, when the door flung open.

A crew member shouted: "We're under attack! It's..." He was cut short by a sword poking through his chest. The blade disappeared and the crew member fell aside, revealing a huge pirate, a bloody sword in his hand and an evil grin on his face.

Jack dove for his sword and readying for battle, still only in his bottoms with no time to put his boots on, but splinters were the farthest from his mind at that point. Daisy had managed to slip out the other side of the bed and put her top on, and was trying very awkwardly to put on her trousers without standing up when the pirate charged at Jack.

Their swords met with a mighty clang. Jack slid backwards, having trouble without boots to grip. The two exchanged blows, each one trying to gain the upper hand, then Jack slipped again. This time he couldn't hold up his guard – the pirate slashed across his left pectoral. Blood poured from the wound. Jack dropped his sword, clutching the wound and stumbling backwards. The pirate moved in for the kill. Just as the sword came down, Jack closed his eyes when a sudden clang made him open them. Looking up he saw Daisy holding a beautiful sword and stopping the pirate just inches from Jack's head. Daisy's face had changed to anger and fury; she pushed the pirate back, parrying the blows that came her way, then with a flick of her wrist, slashed the pirate's throat. He dropped his sword, grabbing the wound. Blood squirted between his fingers as he dropped to his knees before slumping over and hitting his face on the floor. A pool of blood quickly formed around him.

Daisy turned and raced to Jack's side.

"That was impressive... ughhh!" Jack winced in pain. Daisy tore the arm off her top and pushed it into the wound to stop the bleeding. "Where did you get that sword?"

"I hid it on me when you brought me on board, but we can talk more after."

Jack just nodded.

Daisy helped him to his feet and used what she could find to tie the make-shift bandage over the wound. Jack donned his jacket and picked up his sword.

Daisy kissed him. "I love you," she said. "No matter what."

"And I, you." The two of them left the quarters, side by side. The sun was high in the sky. Jack (in between fights) looked around. Parts of the docks were on fire. Then Jack saw it – the enemy ship! And on deck he could just make out the figure and hat from all those years ago...

"Red Beard!" he thought. The fight continued, spilling over from the ship to the docks where Jack, Daisy and his crew fought hordes of pirates. They seemed to be everywhere. The battle continued for hours. Bodies were littered everywhere and the docks had been transformed in to a picture of hell. The streets ran red with blood and the screams of the dying echoed through the alleys. The battle slowly but surely shifted in Jack and his men's favour; the pirates had started to retreat. Jack had already started making his way back to the ship. The *Revenge* was in bad shape – her front mast had been felled and laid across the deck and the hull had at least a dozen holes in it. Cannon trollies had been shattered and the barrels were strewed all over the place. Jack called what men were left to him. "Go into town and round up as many able men as you can find."

"Yes, sir," they said.

The Major, who had been wounded, came up to him. "Sir, this came for you." The major handed Jack the folded piece of paper.

"Thank you. Find the surgeon, get him up here to look at yours and my wounds."

"Yes, sir." The Major hurried off as Jack opened the paper.

"What does it say?" came a voice behind him. Jack looked round – it was Daisy.

"I have been promoted to Vice-Admiral and given charge of this small fleet; that's what these ships are here for."

"That's great news!" she exclaimed.

"It is. Now, where did you learn to fight like that?"

"My father taught me but I don't show it as that's not who I am."

"And that sword – it's beautiful. The ruby in the hilt is stunning."

"My father gave it to me. It was my mother's. She was killed when I was young."

"I'm sorry to hear that."

"Thank you."

"But how did you hide it when being brought on board?"

"Well, nobody checked my back."

Jack smiled and hugged Daisy.

The surgeon came and saw to Jack's wound which wasn't as bad as it looked. The major's was worse; his forearm had been broken. The surgeon did what he could. "If it doesn't heal it will have to be amputated."

The major just nodded.

"Major, have you seen Edward?"

"No, sir."

"That means he will be charged with desertion."

"Yes, sir."

"We must give chase as soon as the men return."

"I wonder why the pirates attacked the port? They have never done this before, sir."

"They are becoming desperate, major. No, you go and rest."

"Yes, sir. Thank you, sir."

Jack turned to Daisy. "Please tell me where your father's hideout is."

"All right, I will tell you. He is on an island, known only as Pena De Muerte, or in English, Death Sentence. It's here." She pointed to an island on a map that Jack had pulled out.

"What sort of force does he have?"

She sighed. "He lives in the abandoned fort at the north end of the island and has at least three hundred men. Before you sank two of them, he had six ships including his flagship. The *Swan* is a razee."

"A razee. What's that?" asked the surgeon who was still tending to the major.

"It's a cut-down, first-rate ship of the line. Faster, but as heavily armed. They just take the top deck off of a first-rate to make a heavily armed frigate," Jack replied. "And we have two frigates: the *London* and the *York*, and a corvette, the *Jamaica*. This will be a close fight," Jack said, "I must speak with the Admiral immediately." Jack marched off to the Admiral's head-quarters.

***

"Congratulations, Vice-Admiral."

"Thank you, sir. I have found where Red Beard is hiding but I need men."

"Your ship is badly damaged."

"That will not be a problem, sir. The *Revenge* will carry the troops and the other ships will protect her."

"Hmm... Sound strategy. All right, take half the garrison with you.

"Thank you, sir." The two of them exchanged salutes and just as Jack was walking out the door the Admiral said, "Good luck and god speed."

Jack took a detour on the way back to the ship to pick up something. When he arrived back at the ship the men were there patching what they could and the other captains had arrived to talk. Jack laid out his plan and the captains all nodded and set off for their own ships. Jack headed for his quarters where Daisy was waiting for him. She came running over to him.

Jack feigned a trip, landing on one knee.

"Are you all right?"

Jack looked up, smiling. In his hand he was holding a ring with a diamond in the centre. "I will be if you say yes to being my wife."

Daisy gasped. "Yes! Yes! I will marry you!"

Jack slipped the ring onto her finger, then getting to his feet, the two shared a kiss.

"But how did you know the size?" she asked.

"When you were asleep I tied a piece of string around your finger then delivered it when we arrived back at port." The two of them hugged.

Chapter 16

The final preparations were being made. What could be fixed, was being fixed. Jack watched as replacement cannons were brought onboard but there was not enough to replace every cannon that had been destroyed. Jack was very happy to see two hundred foot infantry, each one dressed in a red coat and armed with a Brown Bess musket fitted with a bayonet, marching towards the docks. Since the *Revenge* was the most undermanned, she would be carrying most of the soldiers (at least one hundred and fifty) and the remaining fifty split between the two frigates.

It took another day for everything to be readied but finally the ships were ready to depart. The *Revenge* took the lead, followed by the two frigates and the corvette at the back of the column. Winds were good and the ships made good time. The mood on board was good; the men sang while they worked. Jack and Daisy took this time to talk more about their pasts. Jack told Daisy everything that happened the night his village was attacked. Jack teared-up as he went into detail of the fight between him and Red Beard. Daisy comforted him; she had to fight to hold back her own tears. Then she told him about her childhood and that Red Beard hadn't always been as vicious, until her mother died when she was five years old.

The two enjoyed their time together, knowing it could be their last.

After three days of good wind and clear skies, the weather changed: a thick fog rolled in and the ships could barely see each other's lamps, even though they were very close to each other. Orders through flags became impossible, so adjusting speed or heading was out of the question. The ships just moved silently through the slightly choppy waters. Jack stared out over the deck but he couldn't even see the bow. The wind started to pick up and Jack was worried a storm could be moving in and he would not see it until it was upon them. The ships kept going until out of the fog came a black mast.

"Enemy ships!" Jack shouted as two flashes came through the fog. The shots missed, landing either side of the ship with a splash. Jack couldn't order the *Revenge* forward guns to be fired as they had been removed to shore up the broadsides, replacing two destroyed cannons on the starboard side so the Revenge sailed forward into cannon fire. Out of the fog loomed a massive ship.

Daisy called to Jack, "That's the *Swan*."

Jack's face changed. The anger he had harboured for so many years was about to be unleashed on the Swan. "Steady men," Jack called out.

The ships came alongside each other as the guns rang out. This was the first time the *Revenge* was badly outgunned, Jack noticed. After the first broadside the *Swan* started to turn to starboard, "She's trying to get behind us. Hard to starboard!" The wheelman worked hard and the ship started to turn. The Revenge matched the Swan's turn.

Then the fog started to lift and there were three more ships coming towards them. Jack couldn't make out what the other three were as he was focused on the *Swan*.

"Send the signal to attack," Jack called, just as the portside guns thundered to life. The frigates sent back the acknowledgement signal and the battle raged. The other ships had started individual battles with the pirate vessels, cannon fire thundered all around. The smoke had almost become as thick as the fog. The *Revenge* was being battered but she was giving as good as she got.

"Sir we have lost most of our cannons," said a crew member.

"Tell the men to arm themselves."

"Sir?"

"Do it."

"Yes, sir." The crew member scurried back down.

"Load chain-shot!" Jack shouted at the gunners. "Target their masts." Jack knew it wouldn't be long before all the cannons on the starboard side would be gone. "Hard to port," Jack called.

The wheelman again began working furiously and the ship groaned as it changed direction. Jack, knowing there had been very little damage to the port side as the ship had been engaging from the starboard, had timed the turn perfectly. The port cannons were ready loaded with chain-shot and aimed upwards. The *Swan* came in to line and almost simultaneously fired. The shots span through the air, cutting rigging, men and masts. Jack watched as the main mast fell, followed by the rear mast. The *Swan* returned the favour. This time nearly every gun was knocked out!

"Come to port. Ram them!" Jack yelled. The wheelman had a look of horror on his face. "Do it, now!" Jack yelled at him. The ship turned.

"Brace!" Jack shouted. Everyone held onto railings and the base of the masts. The *Revenge* collided with the *Swan* with an almighty crash! Wood snapped, and even though they braced, people were still knocked off their feet.

Jack was the first on to the deck of the *Swan*. His fury could not be contained. Every pirate that stood in his way was cut down where they stood. The soldiers joined in. Musket fire could be heard everywhere. Jack made his way to the captain's quarters. A pirate stood in his way but Jack didn't stop. He didn't even flinch as he pulled out his pistol and fired, hitting the pirate in the chest. The pirate fell to the floor groaning in agony.

Jack looked at him as he walked passed. "Be thankful; I was aiming for your head. Now you will face the noose if you survive."

He kept walking until he reached the door. He kicked it open and there looking out the window was a figure dressed in black and a hat with a long feather in it. Jack walked in, drawing his sword up to chest. Through gritted teeth he said, "Tell me where my sister is."

The figure remained silent. "Turn around and face me!" Jack bellowed. The figure laughed and slowly turned around. Jack's face changed to disbelief as he looked upon the figure's face.

Chapter 17

Jack stared in at the figure. "Edward?" Jack just shook head. "No. Why?"

"Red Beard brought me the men who killed my parents and after I tied cannon balls to their legs and threw them overboard, I thought of you and how you abandoned me. That's why the pirates attacked the dock – to pick me up."

"You've betrayed England, you've betrayed me. Now surrender!"

Edward smiled. "Then we have nothing more to say."

"As you wish." Jack lunged at Edward, their swords clashing like when they were children but this time was for real. The boys who once played together and would do anything to protect each other were now locked in a fight to the death. Neither one willing to give an inch; the two matched each other's moves – every jab was met with a parry, every swipe met with a duck. The two were evenly matched until Edward caught Jack's hand, causing him to drop his sword. Edward moved in, sweeping Jack's legs, but just as Edward was about to strike, Daisy appeared in the doorway, a pistol in her hand.

Jack yelled, "No!" as Daisy fired, hitting Edward in the shoulder. He dropped his sword but that didn't stop him; he came at Jack, who had just got to his feet. Edward struck the first blow, hitting Jack in the stomach. Jack hit Edward under the jaw with his left hand. Edward reeled backwards, then charged Jack, tackling him to the ground. The two hit each other again and again. Edward had blood coming from a cut on his lip, Jack from one on his cheek. Then Jack kicked

Edward backwards and he hit the floor with a thud. When he looked up he saw Jack, sword in hand, the point just millimeters from Edward's throat.

"Go ahead, kill me." Edward said.

Jack's face showed his anger. "No. You may have betrayed England, but you were once my friend and though that may not mean anything to you..." Jack looked down. "It means something to me." Jack thought for a moment. "You'll stand trial for desertion and piracy."

Just then a crew member raced in. "Sir, we have won!" Jack turned his head. "Good. What's the damage to the fleet?"

"The frigates are all right but the corvette is badly damaged; she will have to return to port."

"Very well. Clad this man in irons and put him aboard the corvette."

"Yes, sir."

Jack then turned his head back to Edward. "Stand up," he commanded. Edward complied. The crew member led him out at sword point. Jack then turned towards Daisy, who had moved aside to allow Edward and the crew member to pass. "Thank you for saving me."

"You mean, again?" She laughed.

"Yes, again," Jack said sheepishly. "But be careful. I don't want to lose anyone else I care about."

Daisy walked over to him and cupped his face with one hand. "You won't lose me. You shouldn't worry so much, I can take care of myself."

He put his hands around her waist. "I know you can, you fight almost as good as me." He smiled.

She slapped his chest playfully, "Almost?" she laughed.

"All right, as good as me. Maybe..." he paused.

"Maybe what?" Daisy now had a cheeky smile on her face.

"Better than me," he finished.

She gave him a quick kiss. "Thank you," she chirped.

The two returned to the ship. Jack looked around at the damage. The carpenter that Jack had commandeered for the trip came up to him.

"How's the damage?" Jack asked.

"Bad but she's still sea-worthy."

"Good. Do what you can."

"Will do."

Jack didn't correct him for not calling him 'Sir' as the way they had borrowed his services involved a bag over his head.

***

The ships were reformed and the fleet, lead once again, by the battered *Revenge*, set off for the island. It didn't take long before the island loomed into view. The ships formed into a row and dropped anchor as close as they could get to the shore. The soldiers started rowing ashore.

Jack and Daisy met on the deck. "Well, this is..." Jack began. She took his hand and kissed him.

"No goodbyes. We finish this together," she said.

Jack smiled at her. "You're amazing, you know?" he said.

"I know," Daisy replied cheekily.

The two checked their weapons and then boarded one of the rowing boats. They held hands as they were rowed ashore, looking back at the ship knowing it could be the last time they saw her. On shore, the two watched as the major came ashore.

"Still got two arms, I see," Jack said, reaching out and shaking the major's hand.

"Yes, sir."

"I thought you would still be resting?"

"I wouldn't miss this for all the tea in England, sir."

Jack was happy to see the major, who had become a close ally and friend, still in one piece. It took a while for the troops to all get ashore. They had lost twenty in the fight but one hundred and eighty was still good.

"Lead the way, major," Jack called, as the major formed up the troops into four columns. They all began marching deep into the island.

It was a beautiful island; sandy beaches, a few scattered palm trees, and a grassy hill further inland. The march was easy to start with, no jungle to fight through. It was quiet and Jack was thinking how nice it was, but the fact they hadn't been ambushed or seen anyone was making Jack uneasy.

They stopped to rest at the base of the hill. The soldiers broke out their canteens of water and rations, as nobody had eaten since before the battle. Jack and Daisy had also broken out something to eat.

"Ah, nothing like Royal Navy Biscuits," he said, biting into one.

Daisy tapped hers on her knee. "Do I eat it or throw it?"

Jack finished his mouthful. "Sometimes I don't know, but I haven't broken a tooth yet!" They finished their rations and took the time they had to rest.

They got to the top of the hill after an hour of trekking and looked out. There, just on the other side of a flat grassy plain stood the fort. It wasn't a full star fort but it was substantial; at least eight cannons lined the top of the wall. Jack used his spyglass. "Those cannons seem new but no one is manning them. Stay alert!"

Jack and Daisy followed behind as the soldiers moved forward until they reached a point where the ground dipped towards the fort's main entrance. There, in front of the fort were two-hundred pirates. Swords and muskets ready, they were jeering at the soldiers, and standing behind them Jack could see Red Beard standing there smiling, his fiery ginger beard easily visible in the sun-light – something Jack hadn't seen that fateful night.

Chapter 18

Jack, seeing Red Beard, lurched forward.

Daisy held him back. "No! Think about it – you will not make it to him before those pirates cut you down," she whispered to him.

Jack relaxed a bit looking at her. "You're right," he said reluctantly.

The major walked out in front of the soldiers and turned. "All right men, this is moment you have trained for. Over there is the enemy. You are His Majesty's foot infantry. Defeat to pirates is not an option. No quarter will be given." He turned back towards the pirates. "For England. For the King!" he shouted.

A collective cheer went up from the soldiers and they started spreading out into three lines. Each man checked his musket and fixed their ring bayonets, which allowed them to fire with the bayonet attached. Jack and Daisy drew their swords. Then came the order from the Major: "Forward!" He shouted, waving the men forward then drawing his sword.

The men started forward, followed by Jack and Daisy. As they got closer Daisy noticed movement up on the wall.

"Up there," she shouted, pointing, just as one of the cannons fired.

The ball smashing into the ground, just feet from the front line, showering them with dirt. The soldiers flinched slightly but kept going forward. Then, as if the gates of hell had opened, the rest of the cannons fired dirt and stones flew everywhere. One soldier was hit in the eye by a stone, but even though he was blinded in the left eye, he did not break formation. The line kept moving forward, seemingly unfazed by the earth exploding all around. Then the cannons fell silent. The line stopped.

Seeing the pirates moving towards them, "Get ready!" shouted the major. The first line knelt down readying there muskets. The second and third lines remained standing. "Steady men, steady."

The tension was building with every step the pirates took. The pirates were within range.

"Level!" shouted the major. The soldiers brought their muskets level. "Fire!"

The first two lines fired. The volley of fire killing at least thirty pirates. Then the second line crouched down and the third line fired, that volley killing another ten. The first line was reloading as fast as they could. The pirates, armed with muskets, returned fire, killing five soldiers. Then the second line stood up again; muskets reloaded, the second volley came. Pirates dropped left and right, some just hit in the limbs, fell screaming in pain. The third line got off one more volley before the pirates were upon them. A fierce melee erupted! The perfect lines had turned into individual battles; the clashing of swords on muskets; pirates knocked down were stabbed with bayonets; soldiers were sliced by swords. The once green field now dyed red with blood. Bodies were everywhere.

Jack and Daisy had now gotten stuck in to the fight. Jack was determined to get to Red Beard, cutting down man after man until he came face to face with him. Soldiers and pirates fighting all around them.

"How is the face?" Red Beard teased.

"Fine. How is the arm?" Jack replied.

The two started circling each other, swords ready, Jack's covered in blood, Red Beard's relatively clean.

"Losing your touch," Jack remarked, looking at Red Beard's sword.

Red Beard snarled and lunged at Jack; their swords locked together. For Jack, the battle around seemed to slow down – he could barely hear the noise, just faint sound of his and Red Beard's breathing. Jack shoved Red Beard backwards, slashing at him, his sword cutting through Read Beard's jacket, failing though to cut the skin. Red Beard looked at the cut, but just as he was about to say something Jack came at him again. The words of William Button ringing in his ears: "Don't let the hatred of Red Beard consume you."

He remained calm, his face almost emotionless. This time, Jack targeted Red Beard's open jacket. As only a thin white top covered his chest, his sword found its mark, cutting through Red Beard's top and opening a long wound across his chest. Red Beard recoiled in pain putting his hand to the wound. Jack moved in. Then Red Beard threw dirt at Jack's face. Jack put his hands up to block and when he put them back down he saw Red Beard turn and run for the fort. Jack gave chase.

"Jack!" Daisy called out, but Jack didn't hear. She began running after the both of them, killing two pirates that tried to stop her.

Red Beard pounded on the doors. "Open up, you mangy dogs!" he shouted. The doors opened with a creak and Red Beard stumbled through. "Close it, quick" he shouted. Two pirates ran to close the door but froze.

"What's wrong with you?" Red Beard snarled, turning and looking at the two pirates who now had their hands up then they started to back up.

"What are you two dogs doing? I will boil you in oil for this!"

"I don't think you will."

Red Beard noticed a sword coming into view, "He only has a sword – get him!"

Jack came into view. In his right hand, his sword, in his left, his pistol. "I would have thought your arm would have remembered this," he said as he wiggled it at the two pirates, beckoning them outside.

"Ah… I had forgotten. It's been so long. Tell me, how is your mother?"

Jack's face changed to anger.

"Oh. Did I hit a nerve?" Red Beard smiled.

Jack walked in to the fort's courtyard. Red Beard was standing by a building at the edge. Daisy entered the fort coming to the side of Jack.

"Ah! My lost daughter returns."

"Lost? You abandoned me to die!" she shouted, her voice laced with a deep hatred. This time it was Jack who had to stop her charging in recklessly.

"Oh, you two are together. How nice, I too have a young woman in my life. Come out, daughter," he beckoned to an open door. Jack and Daisy looked as a young woman stepped out from the building. The sun caught her dark black hair.

"Hello, sister," she said. Jack squinted, then his eyes opened wide with shock: he noticed the features – though older, he still recognised her face.

"Hello yourself. Still father's favourite?" Daisy said back to her. Jack couldn't believe his eyes.

"Yes. He has taught me to be a better swordsman than you will ever be."

"Ha! We will see." Daisy then saw Jack's face, "What is it?"

Jack said, "That's my little sister."

"What?" she gasped.

"That's Elizabeth, my little sister she was…"

"Taken. Yes. That night when I burnt down your village and slaughtered your mother, and have I forgotten something?

Oh! Yes... then slowly tainted your friendship with, what was his name, oh yes, Edward."

Jack raised his pistol, aiming for Red Beard's heart.

"Ah, ah, ahhh..." Red Beard waggled his finger at him. "Lizzie, have you ever seen this man before?"

Elizabeth looked hard at Jack. "No, Father," she said.

"Elizabeth, it's me! Jack, your brother!" Jack said, pleading in his mind for her to remember.

"My name is Lizzie and I have never seen you before."

"You see, I was going to sell her but then I thought what better than to turn her in to the daughter I never had?" Red Beard said, very proud of what he had just said. "Now, be a good girl and kill Daisy."

Elizabeth drew her sword, "With pleasure, Father."

Jack took Daisy's hand. She looked at him.

"Please don't kill my sister," Jack whispered.

"Don't worry, I won't, but I will knock her out." Daisy replied, a sly smile on her face. The four started to advance towards each other. Red Beard waved his fingers in the air and the fort's doors closed. Jack turned his head slightly and caught a glimpse of another pirate putting a bar across the doors.

"Just to make sure this is a fair fight. Don't want your soldier friends spoiling the party," Red Beard said, smiling.

Chapter 19

Red Beard turned and whispered, "Make her suffer," in Elizabeth's ear.

She nodded then smiled at Daisy. "Let's see how weak being with this navy dog has made you," she said.

Daisy gritted her teeth, silence engulfed the courtyard with only the faint sounds of battle outside to be heard. It felt like an eternity, yet only lasted seconds before Elizabeth charged at Daisy. At the same time Jack charged at Red Beard. Their swords clashed at the same time; the clang echoed around the fort and could even be heard outside. Jack's face was solemn as he stared into Red Beard's eyes. Red Beard kicked Jack backwards but Jack quickly regained his balance, just in time to parry Red Beard's slash. The two kept trading blows.

Daisy and Elizabeth's fight was more even; the two holding the other's sword arm up, their strength evenly matched. Daisy kicked Elizabeth in the crotch, sending her reeling back.

"Who is the weak one now?" Daisy said smugly, walking to the hunched over Elizabeth and grabbing her by the hair, pulling her up and punching her in the jaw. Then she let her guard down as she saw Jack and Red Beard's fight, allowing Elizabeth to regain her composure and kick Daisy in the stomach and slash her across the arm. Daisy screamed out in pain – Jack looked over at Daisy, which gave Red Beard an opening, slashing Jack's right arm. Blood stained Jack's jacket but he didn't flinch. He returned the favour, slashing the opposite arm of Red Beard. Blood ran down his arm.

The battle continued for an hour. Jack, now determined to finish the battle pulled out his pistol and fired, but the ball missed. Jack threw down his pistol and lunged at Red Beard who dodged out the way. As Jack's back was turned Red Beard span around and pulled out his pistol and fired; the ball hit Jack in the right shoulder. Jack yelled in pain, dropping his sword. Daisy, who had locked swords with Elizabeth, looked as the shot was fired.

"No!" she screamed as Jack dropped to his knees. Elizabeth, seeing an opportunity, stabbed Daisy in the left shoulder. She dropped to her knees, a look of pain painted across her face. She turned her head and looked at Jack, a tear in her eyes. Jacks turned his head and looked at her. As their eyes met they smiled at each other, knowing that if this is it they will be together forever. Jack, on his knees, turned around and looked at Red Beard who had an evil grin on his face. He walked over and bent down, grabbing Jack's face and whispered, "Before I kill you I want you to watch as your little sister kills the love of your life."

Jack smiled, a twinkle in his eye. "There is something you should know," he said. He slowly felt around with his left hand until he felt the hilt of his sword.

"And, what's that?"

"I trained with both hands!"

Red Beard's smile disappeared as Jack raised his left arm, holding the sword like a knife and plunged it into Red Beard's right shoulder. Red Beard yelled out in pain, dropping his sword. As Jack slowly got to his feet, Red Beard looked up, still hunched over in pain, Jack grabbed his head and brought up his knee flooring Red Beard. Jack then walked over and put his boot on Red Beard's chest, retrieved his sword and pointed it at the unconscious Red Beard. In his mind he contemplated driving his sword through his chest.

"Please, don't!" called Daisy.

Jack looked over at her, she was clutching her left shoulder blood, seeping from the wound. Elizabeth stood over her.

"Just let it go," Daisy said.

"But he took everything from me," Jack replied.

"But he didn't take me."

Jack thought, then turned. "Lizzie, touch her and I swear, after I cut out your father's heart, I will kill you!" Jack was holding back tears as he spoke but knew Elizabeth would come at him. And she did.

"I will kill both of you!" she said as she lunged at Jack, who, though looking awkward, parried her with the sword in his left hand. The two matched each other, parry after parry, then they locked swords. Jack was pale as he had lost a lot of blood. He looked into Elizabeth's eyes and he remembered their childhood; he saw the little sister he had promised his mother he'd protect, who was now hell bent on ending him. He pushed her back but started feeling weak. He blocked her next attack and then the two locked once more. This time Elizabeth pushed the sword closer and closer towards Jack's face. Then just as she was about to cut his face, a hand grabbed her shoulder.

"Don't you hurt him!" snarled Daisy. Jack took this distraction and knocked the sword from Elizabeth's hand. Then Daisy turned her around, using only her right hand and punched Elizabeth in the face before kicking her legs out from under her. Elizabeth hit the ground with a thud. Then, just as she was about to get up, Daisy kicked her around the face, knocking her unconscious.

Daisy and Jack took each other's hand.

"I thought I was going to lose you," Jack said.

"Me too," replied Daisy. The two shared a quiet moment but it wasn't long before they were interrupted by a thudding on the doors. They got ready fearing, the worst but when the doors crashed open in came the red coated sailors.

"Thank God, you too made it!" came a voice – it was the major.

"Good to see you, too" said Jack.

The soldiers flooded the courtyard. They trained their muskets on Red Beard and Elizabeth. Red Beard came to first as Jack walked over to him. "I said I would get you."

Red Beard stayed silent. He was hauled to his feet and placed in irons.

"What should we do with him, sir?" asked one soldier.

Jack looked at Daisy. "Take him to the ship. We will bring him back to England and there he will stand trial."

"Yes, sir." The soldiers hauled him away. Then Elizabeth came to and she was helped up. Daisy walked up to her.

"This is for trying to take the love of my life from me." And she punched Elizabeth in the nose.

"Argh!" shouted Elizabeth.

"And, what about this one, sir?"

"She will also be returning to England" said Jack, sadly, as Elizabeth was taken away. Daisy walked up and kissed Jack with such passion that he blushed. The two embraced each other, forgetting their wounds.

"Ow!" they said in unison.

"Sorry," said Jack.

"Don't be silly," replied Daisy, smiling. And with that they followed the soldiers who were leading Red Beard and Elizabeth out of the fort. Jack and Daisy looked at the carnage left behind after the battle; the injured limped away with help. Pirate prisoners, under gun point, were clearing away and burying the dead. The smoke finally clearing.

The surgeon came ashore to treat the injured on the beach. Jack and Daisy held each other's hands as their wounds were stitched and cauterized.

Chapter 20

The ships arrived back at Kingston. Jack and Daisy went ashore. Daisy was now wearing the ring Jack had given her. They made their way to the admiral's head-quarters. Jack kissed Daisy, a smile on his face. She waited outside as he entered. The Admiral was smiling, "Jack," he boomed.

"Yes, sir?" Jack replied, thinking he had done something wrong.

"Congratulations are in order, my boy! Wiping out the pirate fleet and capturing the notorious Red Beard."

"Thank you, sir."

"Word of what you have done has spread far and wide and I am sending a letter to the king himself and recommending you for the rank of vice-admiral."

Jack smiled. "Thank you, sir. We will be heading for England by weeks end to deliver Red Beard."

"Very good. I wish I could be there to see him hang." The admiral paused. Standing up and extending his hand, Jack took it. "I hope one day to see you again. You have been a superb officer. Commodore Button would have been proud."

Jack stood proud, holding back tears of joy for a change. "Thank you, sir. It has been a pleasure."

The two saluted each other. Jack then turned and left. He met Daisy outside, still smiling.

"Is everything all right?" she asked

"Yes, my love. For the first time in years everything is perfect." And he took her hand and the two went to the jail where Edward was being held. Jack approached the head jailer.

"Bring out Edward," he said.

"Sir, what for?"

"He is being taken back to England. There he will stand trial in front of the admiralty for his crimes."

"Yes, sir." Then the jailer disappeared for a few minutes. When he returned, Edward was behind him his hands bound in irons, a guard on each side.

"Take him to the *Revenge*'s brig. I will follow shortly," Jack said to the guards.

"Yes, sir," they replied, and marched Edward away. Edward kept his head down, not looking at Jack.

Jack and Daisy spent their first night ashore lying on the beach together looking up at the stars. They had enjoyed a picnic and wine by candle light.

"I didn't know you could be so romantic," said Daisy as she rested her head on Jack's chest. Jack cringed slightly as the wound on his chest still ached,

"You will find I am full of surprises!" he replied, smiling. And the two fell asleep. The air was warm; a gentle breeze blowing but otherwise the night was still and calm.

***

They awoke early and slowly returned to the ship. Edward was already on-board, as Jack and Daisy came onboard, the Major came up to them.

"Sir, it's good to see you in high spirits."

"It's good to see you too, my friend." And the two shook hands. The major smiled then went about his business. The ships got underway at noon, the *Revenge*, again, leading the way.

A day into the trip, Jack went down to see Elizabeth in the brig. He opened the door and went inside. She was sitting down with her head in her hands.

"Hello," Jack said. Elizabeth looked up. "I never thought when you were taken that I would see you again," he said.

"Taken? No, my Mother..."

"Was killed by Red Beard's men that night you were taken, and he gave me this." Jack pointed at his face. Elizabeth remained silent. "Here, I hope this will make you remember," said Jack.

He pulled Elizabeth's shield that she lost that night out of his pocket and placed it beside her. Elizabeth looked as Jack got up to leave. On his way out he heard Elizabeth whisper, "Thank you, Jack." Jack didn't turn but he did smile as he hadn't told her his name.

On his way out of the brig, the guard stopped him. "Sir, the prisoner Edward has asked for you."

"Thank you."

Jack then went into Edward's cell. "You asked for me?" he said.

"Yes. I wanted to say I'm sorry for what I did. And that I saw her."

"Did you know?"

"What? That Red Beard had your sister? No, when I found out I felt even worse. The way I had treated you and taken our friendship for granted. I am happy for you and Daisy."

"Thank you. I will do what I can but I can't promise anything."

Edward smiled at him. "That's more than I deserve."

"It is all I can do for an old friend."

"Do you think things between us will ever be back to how it was?"

Jack's face changed. "I don't think so, but I do hope with time we can be friends again."

"I would like that."

Jack then turned and left.

***

The ships arrived in Portsmouth a day later. People were cheering on the docks. News of the capture had spread to every corner of the Empire. As the ships moored, Jack and Daisy came ashore, followed by soldiers leading Edward and Elizabeth. Then from the frigate came Red Beard. Jack and Daisy stood at the bottom of the ramp smiling. Edward was taken to the local jail with Elizabeth. Red Beard was taken to Newgate prison in London.

***

Jack attended the hearing of Edward first.

"Edward Rosely, you are charged with desertion and piracy. How do you plead?"

Edward stood and said, "Guilty, Your Honour." Jack then stood.

"Your Honour, may I say something?"

The judge looked. "What is it, vice-admiral?"

"Your Honour, Edward was my dearest friend and I feel his actions were caused by severe trauma at seeing his parents murdered. And the stress of trying to find the man responsible."

The judge thought for a while then said, "Very well. I have heard of what happened, but that does still not excuse the crime. Because of the Vice-Admiral's testimony, I am sentencing you to five years in prison then a further five years in the colonies." And he banged his gavel.

Before Edward was taken away he turned to Jack and said, "Thank you."

It would be two more days before Elizabeth's trial and a month before Red Beard's so Jack and Daisy spent that time planning their wedding. They had decided to wait until after Red Beard's sentencing.

At Elizabeth's trial, Jack stood and said: "Please. I lost my sister once, don't take her away again."

The Judge came to a verdict quickly. "Due to the circumstances and what has transpired, I am sentencing you to one year in an asylum. Then you will be handed over to the care of your brother for three years." The gavel banged down and Elizabeth looked at Jack and smiled. He smiled back.

***

Jack took Daisy to the remains of his village.

"So, this is where you were born and raised."

"Yes, And now I have a surprise for you."

"What is it?"

"This." Jack pointed to where his house had once stood. "I bought the land where my parent's house once stood and I thought I would have a house built for us."

"Oh, Jack! That's wonderful!" she exclaimed and kissed Jack.

The house was underway when Jack and Daisy left for London. When they arrived Daisy went to the best dress maker in the country for her wedding dress and Jack was summoned to the admiralty.

"Jack, for your service and devotion to duty, and for the apprehension of the notorious pirate, Red Beard, I am proud to give you the promotion to Admiral. Congratulations" said the first Sea Lord.

"Thank you, sir," Jack could barely contain his joy.

"And the king would like to see you and your wife to be."

"Yes, sir."

Jack met Daisy and told her the good news. The two embraced and went to the old bailey where Red Beard's trial was due to begin. The court was packed with news men writing down everything and sketching portraits of Red Beard.

The judge spoke first: "John Maylor, also known as Red Beard, you are charged with murder; piracy; kidnapping; attacking His Majesty's ships and arson. How do you plead?"

Red Beard smirked. "All right, you got me. I'm guilty of it all and I don't regret a thing. In fact, God could give me a second chance and I would do the same."

There was commotion in the courtyard, people muttering amongst each other.

"Order, order! I say!" shouted the judge, repeatedly banging his gavel. "Jury, what say you?"

In unison the jury cried out, "Guilty!"

The Judge looked at Red Beard. "John Maylor, you have been found guilty and I…"

"Blah, blah, blah, just get this over with," interrupted Red Beard.

"Sentence you to two months in prison, then, in front of the king, you are to be hanged by the neck until you are dead." The judge banged his gavel. Red Beard was hauled off and Jack and Daisy left together.

"It's finally over," Jack said as he breathed a sigh of relief.
"Yes it is and now we can start our life together."

The next day they met the king at the Tower of London. Jack bowed as the king approached, and Daisy curtsied in her new dress.

"Rise, please," said the king kindly, "For your services in defense of this kingdom, kneel." Jack knelt. The king was given his sword. "I knight you: Sir Jack Leighton. Arise." Then the king turned to Daisy. "And for you, I give you, for your wedding, the use of Westminster Abbey."

"Thank you, your majesty," Daisy said, holding back her excitement. And with that the King retreated into his palace and Jack and Daisy left.

The next day the bells rang as Jack and Daisy were married. Daisy wore a beautiful long white dress and Jack wore his finest uniform, now decorated with two medals.

"In the presence of almighty God, I now pronounce you man and wife. You may kiss the bride."

Jack lifted Daisy's veil and kissed her. The two turned and, holding each other's hands, walked down the aisle. Outside there was a massive crowd waiting and when Jack and Daisy came out the bells rang and the crowd cheered. Then they got in the waiting carriage and they set off for their new home.

***

A month later Jack was sitting outside his now finished house when Daisy came out, "I have news."

"What news?"

Daisy smiled, putting her hands on her stomach. "I am with child."

Jack embraced her, "That's wonderful news!"

Then a messenger arrived. "This is for you, sir." He handed Jack a letter.

"Thank you." Jack opened it, his face changing.

"What is it?" asked Daisy. Jack showed her the letter. It read:

You think your prison can hold me? Red Beard.

"He is just trying to ruin our peace."

Jack looked at her with a worried look. "I sure hope so, my love."

The two of them held each other. Daisy let go of the paper and watched as it floated away in the breeze.